He'd neve...
before...

Really, what was the big deal? Jason thought. So he and Christy had been dreaming about each other. They were right in the middle of the sex-all-the-time part of their relationship. Of course they'd dream about each other.

But the *exact* same dream? That wasn't possible. Then again, it kind of explained why he'd had a dream about being a spa guy. A *naked* spa guy. That was obviously Christy's contribution.

Jason grinned when he thought about that, choosing to focus on the fact that she thought he was hot. That she'd thought he was hot before they'd officially met. That was cool. Still...

God, he needed a run.

He ran. He swam. He saw his therapist, to whom he said absolutely nothing about his dreams. He was freaked out, but he wasn't stupid. Talking about shared dreams would be career suicide, especially in the military. They did however, talk about Christy and what was going on between them.

In the end, Jason agreed with the doc: women were good. Sex was good. He should stop worrying and just enjoy it.

Which worked out great...until he met her for dinner later.

Dear Reader,

I have a friend who puts great stock in her dreams. She considers them messages from beyond. Me? I think my dreams are the flotsam and jetsam of my mind, pulling random stuff together and presenting them as a story because that's what I do. I put stories together from random stuff.

But once, I had an erotic dream. Okay, okay, maybe not so much an erotic dream as a dream about a facial that I was getting for my birthday. But by the time I woke up, I had this great idea about a couple of strangers sharing hot dreams. I mean, do you actually confess to the stranger, "Hey I had this great dream about you last night"? Heck no! So how long before you fess up? How intimate do you get in the real world before the dream world makes an appearance?

When I told my friend about it, she asked me to think about what purpose those images could have. What is the underlying message in a series of erotic dreams? From there, well, *Night After Night...* was born.

I hope you enjoy your nights as much as Christy and Jason do!

Best,

Kathy Lyons

Kathy Lyons

NIGHT AFTER NIGHT...

TORONTO NEW YORK LONDON
AMSTERDAM PARIS SYDNEY HAMBURG
STOCKHOLM ATHENS TOKYO MILAN MADRID
PRAGUE WARSAW BUDAPEST AUCKLAND

Recycling programs
for this product may
not exist in your area.

ISBN-13: 978-0-373-79683-0

NIGHT AFTER NIGHT...

www.Harlequin.com

Printed in U.S.A.

ABOUT THE AUTHOR

A *USA TODAY* bestselling author, Kathy Lyons has made her mark with sizzling romances. She adores unique settings, wild characters and erotic, exotic love. And if she throws in a dragon or a tigress here and there, it's only in the name of fun! An author of more than 30 novels, she adores the fabulousness that is Blaze. She calls them her sexy treat and hopes you find them equally delicious. Kathy loves hearing from readers. Visit her at www.kathylyons.com or find her on Facebook and Twitter under her other pen name, Jade Lee.

Books by Kathy Lyons

HARLEQUIN BLAZE
535—UNDER HIS SPELL
576—TAKING CARE OF BUSINESS
599—IN GOOD HANDS

To get the inside scoop on Harlequin Blaze and its talented writers, be sure to check out blazeauthors.com.

All backlist available in ebook. Don't miss any of our special offers. Write to us at the following address for information on our newest releases.

Harlequin Reader Service
U.S.: 3010 Walden Ave., P.O. Box 1325, Buffalo, NY 14269
Canadian: P.O. Box 609, Fort Erie, Ont. L2A 5X3

1

CHRISTY BAKER WAS HAVING a great dream. She knew it was a dream because when, honestly, would a hot marine step into an esthetician's room and start giving her a facial? Especially since he wasn't wearing any clothes.

Yowza! Ever since she'd hit puberty while living on a military base, she'd had fantasies about soldiers. Didn't matter what branch of the military so long as they were half-naked and ripped. And as she got older, the "half" part of naked disappeared.

Hence the awesome dream right now of a naked marine gently slathering sea-something onto her face. She was lying on a heated, cushioned table while he slowly stroked therapeutic mud onto her face and her toes curled in delight. Then she let out a purr of appreciation. It was a dream, right? She could purr if she wanted to. He looked down at her, his blue eyes sparkling with humor.

"So you like this stuff, huh?"

"Come over this way." She reached for his bulging bicep and tugged him down by the side of the table.

He complied, and oh, yes, ripped abs, sculpted torso, and a cute dimple in his left cheek. Sadly, she couldn't see the lower half of his body, but she was sure it was equally impressive.

"Much better," she said.

"You know this is a full-body treatment, right?" he said, flashing that dimple again.

"Of course it is," she said. Because this was an awesome dream.

"Then just close your eyes and relax. Let me do all the work."

"I leave myself in your capable hands," she crooned as she closed her eyes and gave herself up to the experience. Except, of course, it wasn't nearly as much fun without the view, so she opened them a moment later.

He was by the sink, his back to her and his buttocks in full display. Was that a tattoo of a swallow on his hip? It didn't matter. The tat just made him all the more mouthwatering.

He was mixing the mud, and she caught a flash of his large hands in and out of stuff that looked like rich, dark chocolate. Soon those hands and that stuff would be all over her body. Best. Dream. Ever.

He must have known she was watching, because he looked over his shoulder at her and flashed her a wink. "This will take just a second. The best stuff comes when you're fully ready."

She was ready. Any more ready and this dream would have a premature ending. Better to focus on something else. Like his narrow waist. The ripples in his back as he worked. "Listen to those kids," she said. "Don't they sound like they're having fun?"

What? Where had that question come from? And

yeah, there were kids laughing and cheering in the background. Probably a playground nearby. But what did that have to do with her full-body treatment?

He tilted his head, obviously listening for something. A frown appeared between his brows, and his eyes grew distant. Worse, he stopped kneading the dark chocolate mixture and she felt she was losing her grip on him.

"Stop thinking so hard!" she cried to bring him back to her. "We were doing something here." She hated it when her dreams spun off in the wrong direction.

He blinked and focused on her. He had turned to face her again, but she still didn't get a look at his body. Not the full frontal, but that was okay. He was carrying the bowl of the chocolate mixture over to her side and his eyes no longer had that distant, slightly lost look. Right now he was zeroing in on her. Well, her breasts actually, which were abruptly uncovered for his viewing.

Any other time she might have felt self-conscious. She had nice breasts. Round, full, *large*. She tended toward the plump side of life anyway. So if this were real life, she'd be covering up the pounds and praying that he wasn't repulsed.

But this was the best dream ever because when he looked at her, his eyes gleamed. He liked what he saw. He wanted what he saw. And whatever bit of self-consciousness that lived in this dream faded away from the delight in his eyes.

"So, I'm supposed to spread this all over?" he asked.

She nodded. "That's what happens in full-body treatments. It's to purify and soften the skin. And since I have skin everywhere…"

"I better make sure to cover every inch."

She continued playing along. "It's important that I get my money's worth. This is a top-end spa."

"Is that what this is?" he asked, as he looked around curiously.

"I'm sure you wouldn't work anywhere but in the best places."

He let loose an outright burst of laughter. "Actually, I work in the worst pits on the planet."

She waved his statement away. "That's your day job. This is your night job." She steadfastly ignored the bright sunlight and the sound of kids' laughter outside. "Right now, you're here with me in a luxury spa and I'm waiting for my treatment."

He smiled at her and wasn't that a megawatt doozy? It wasn't that his teeth gleamed or anything. It was just a warm, fun smile like you might get from the guy next door. Especially if the guy who lived next door was hot and naked and intent on touching every part of your body.

"Do I start at your face and work down? Or go straight for the gold?"

"Your choice. I'm easy." She could be easy in a dream, right? So the double entrendre was exactly what she meant.

He scooped out some of the mixture and squished it between his hands. His eyes never left hers as he worked, and as much as she wanted to watch the play of muscles on his chest, she couldn't force herself to look away from his beautiful blue eyes.

And then he was finally, blessedly, done with mixing and got down to the stroking. He started on her neck, putting on the chocolate with long strokes that went from her chin down to the tops of her breasts. Wow, that felt good. Like heat and sweetness being rubbed gently into her body. How she could taste the sweetness of him, she didn't know, but that was the beauty of dreams.

She released a low, throaty purr. He smiled and that dimple flashed at her.

"I love that sound," he said.

"I love what you're doing to make me make that sound."

Oh, why couldn't she be suddenly witty for just once? Fortunately, her marine esthetician didn't seem to mind. Instead, he leaned forward and kissed her eyes closed, first the left, then the right.

The scent of him was *perfect!* Her eyelids stayed shut to appreciate the deliciousness of it.

And then his hands found her breasts.

He shaped her, he stroked her, he thumbed across her nipples while her purr dropped to a huskier octave. Okay, so she loved it when a guy spent a long time on her breasts. She loved it even better when he began licking her nipples, sucking them to a point, and sometimes a little nip here and there would send her to the moon.

He did it all. Before she knew it—before she wanted it—she was grabbing his massive shoulders and coming with a cry!

Which woke her right up. *Damn!* That was one dream she would have loved to stay with for a while. For a long while.

She rubbed her eyes and stretched, hearing herself purr for real. The ripples were still going, though they were fading too quickly. Still that had been a great dream. Hawaii must be having a beneficial effect on her psyche.

She lay in bed, just appreciating the luxury of the new environment. It wasn't that she was living in a resort or anything. Traveling Officer Quarters, or TOQ, at Pearl Harbor Navel Station were not high living by any standards. But it was a *different* location than her Cincinnati apartment, and a *different* job than a kindergarten teacher in an Ohio public school. She was a summer tutor for kids stationed at the naval base. For Christy, that meant a paid summer in Hawaii. Who wouldn't want that?

It's not that she didn't enjoy her regular life in Ohio, but she'd gotten the feeling lately that she was stuck in a rut. She hung out with the same people every day, ate the same food, did the same things. Every day. Her friends and colleagues all knew about her and her very military family, knew that she suffered from chronic joint pain, and knew that she struggled every day to walk and move like a normal person. She never tried anything new because everyone tried to stop her. They were afraid she'd hurt herself. So she gave in and never challenged herself or anyone else. Until the day she heard about the opening at Pearl Harbor. A place far from Ohio where no one knew her at all.

Despite the objections from her family, she'd applied and gotten the job. For this summer only, she was a summer tutor in Hawaii. She taught English in a classroom on base from ten to noon Monday through Friday, plus she had private sessions with about a dozen kids. It was a great job and one she was well qualified to do. Better yet, no one knew her here. No one knew that her joints might swell up and make her walk like the Tin

Man who'd been out in the rain all day. She was just Miss Baker, summer tutor and English teacher. Perfect and blessedly *anonymous*. She could do whatever she wanted, be whomever she wanted, and experiment however she chose.

After this summer, she'd reevaluate. Did she want her old life back in Ohio? Or was it time for a bigger, better, more sweeping change? So, simple steps. A little exploration in Hawaii where no one could baby her. And no one would stop her. If it worked out, then maybe she'd make a bigger change after the summer.

She got out of bed slowly, smiling because life was just that good this morning. It helped that her joints didn't hurt so much. She didn't know if it was because of the change in climate or her dream, but either way was good with her. Chronic joint pain was something she'd lived with her entire life. Sometimes it was just her knees and hips that ached. Sometimes it was her whole body. Drugs helped—some. Rest helped—some. Mostly, it just was. Some days were fine, some days were painful, and some were just agony. She never knew what to expect. So this morning's dream plus a lack of pain made everything in Hawaii feel rosy and new.

Her calendar flashed her a morning motto of: embrace the unexpected gift. She thought that was especially appropriate today. Then it was a shower and a sundress. Her first tutoring appointment wasn't until nine, so she had a little bit of time.

Her hair was still wrapped in a towel when she walked barefoot into the kitchenette. The Traveling Officer's Quarters (TOQ) was built like a low-budget motel. Her room had a bed, a desk, a television and a bathroom. Plus one other thing: a connecting door that led to a kitchenette that was shared with whoever held the room next door. It was a galley kitchen, barely big enough for two people standing sideways. But she had a box of Froot Loops and a coffeemaker in there, and she went right to work on her breakfast of champions.

She had a spoonful of cereal halfway to her mouth when her kitchen-mate walked in. She'd been told when she moved in that she'd be sharing with someone, and she hadn't given it much thought. She'd had roommates before. No biggie.

That is, until she looked up. Milk dribbled from her spoon to her bowl as her half-naked marine esthetician stumbled toward the coffee.

2

CAPT. JASON WHITE WAS FACED with a no-win situation. He could turn tail and run, never a good option in his opinion. Or he could go for the coffee and face the subject of his weirdest erotic dream.

He had never wanted to be one of those metro guys who dressed fashionably and talked manicures. So why the hell had he dreamed he was giving a facial to his kitchen-mate? Not that it had been a bad thing. Turns out the chestnut-haired schoolteacher had bombshell breasts and he had gotten off on doing wonderful things with them. So had she, apparently, but he felt a little cheated that his own wet dream had stopped before the glorious finish. At least from his perspective. He didn't mind being gentlemanly in real life. In fact, he insisted on it. But in the privacy of his own nighttime fantasies, he wanted his fair share.

But now he was standing right in front of the object of his most lustful fantasy. And worse, she was wearing a sundress that hinted at the glory of her breasts but didn't actually confirm anything. And damn it, he wanted to know if what he'd dreamed was anything like the reality.

"Uh, good morning," she said over her bowl of cereal as she hastily stepped back to give him room. Given the galley kitchenette, there really wasn't anywhere for her to go, and she backed straight into the refrigerator. Her face was flushed, probably from her shower. And the towel that wrapped her hair started to tilt as it bumped the freezer handle. "Oh!" she gasped as she reached up to grab the towel. But in her hand she had a full bowl of Froot Loops, which was beginning to slosh.

He reacted on instinct. He grabbed her bowl, keeping it from spilling, but also wrapping his hand around one of hers. She had lovely hands, the fingers long and elegant but with blunt, unpolished nails that didn't stab him. Her free hand went up to brace the towel, but it was too late. The thing came undone and her wet hair tumbled down.

Again, he just reacted. He caught the towel with his other hand, and then they were standing there, both of them with one hand on a bowl of cereal and the other on a wet towel. And all he could think was that she was close enough to kiss.

He watched her gaze dip to his chest and back up, and he knew she was thinking the same thing. He wasn't vain or anything, but some things were obvious. He was just wearing a pair of shorts and after being blown sky-high in the Philippines, he'd lost a stone in weight. That left him thinner and weaker, but also gave him muscle definition like never before. In fact, his sister had asked if he could pose for her Men of the Military calendar. He'd declined that offer, but he wasn't about to say no to his living erotic dream.

Too bad the woman wasn't asking. She was just thinking, and as a gentleman and an officer, he just couldn't make the first move. Not to a near stranger. So he opted for a simple "Good morning."

"Sorry," she muttered, trying to shy backward even farther though there was nowhere to go. "I'm such a klutz. Especially in the morning."

"You weren't being klutzy. It was the towel's fault." And so saying, he lifted the bowl from her hand to set on the counter. She went for the towel and pushed the wet hair out of her eyes.

"Dumb towels! Always getting in the way."

"They're a menace," he said, nodding gravely though his lips were twitching. She made him want to smile, and given his past month, that was beyond incredible. Sadly, the humor faded as they both just stood there staring. She had beautiful eyes. Rich, brown and large, but there were crinkles on either side of them that told him she smiled a lot.

Lust slammed through him hard. From the moment his friend had given him the details on his new kitchenmate, he'd known he was in trouble. He'd learned she was a hot, single kindergarten teacher, and since he'd always had a wholesome-girl fantasy, a sexy dream was the next logical step. He got off on the girl next door with the easy laugh. Given his rough childhood, he hadn't known many girls who fit that profile. And here she was, standing before him like a Christmas present, waiting to be opened by him. Or so his libido believed.

Meanwhile, her blush was growing deeper, painting the skin of her chest a rosy hue. "Um, I'm sorry if I woke you," she said. "I'm Christy Baker. I'm here for a few months to help with summer tutoring."

"Yeah, I know. I saw you when you moved in and my buddy in housing mentioned it to me." He didn't mention that his buddy Mac had probably handpicked Miss Baker as his kitchen-mate for a not so ethical reason. Mac thought Jason desperately needed to get laid. Given his reaction to her, he couldn't really argue. Jason held out his hand. "I'm Jason White. I'm here to… I'm here for a while. Hopefully not long."

He was here on indefinite medical leave while the docs tried to get him to remember his last mission. There was something really important right there at the edge of his very messed up memory that he knew he had to get to. But it remained a stubborn blank wall. So he remained here.

"Um," she said again, her blush reheating. "I've really got to get to school. Got a new student…"

It took him a second to realize she wanted out of the kitchenette. Well, of course she did. He probably looked really scary, some scarred-up stranger staring at her. He rubbed a hand over his face. "Right. Sorry." He backed out of the tiny galley. "Can't think right now."

"Go ahead and take the rest of the coffee. I always make too much."

"No such thing," he said automatically. But that wasn't the reason for his confusion. No, it was because all his blood was down south of his brain.

He backed up far enough that she didn't have to touch him as she scooted out of the galley. But it wasn't far enough to keep his lust in check. He got a full view of her profile, and damn, yes, there were those bombshell breasts bound in some iron-tight women's bra. But what hit him just as hard was her scent. Clean and sweet. Some herbal shampoo and fresh water. No perfumes, no sweat, just clean, sweet woman. It was all he could do to stand there and not drag her into his cave-man home.

Fortunately, he didn't have to wait long. She was ducking into her room and quietly shutting the door before he lost control of his inner Neanderthal. Sadly, it didn't help much. The flimsy door and the equally frail lock would be no match for him if he ever descended into real caveman mode.

The problem was that Miss Bombshell School-teacher was not a summer fling kind of girl. She was the marrying kind, and that made her strictly off-limits. He didn't miss the irony that all those things that made her off-limits were the exact reasons he wanted her so badly. Completely aside from his girl-next-door fantasy, he'd just turned thirty last month. That was old enough to stop wanting to run around swamps looking for bad guys and start thinking about living stateside with a wife and kids.

But whereas Miss Christy would make a great wife and mother, he would make a lousy husband and father. Not with this hole in his memory and the nagging feeling that lives were at stake because he couldn't get his brain to work right. His unit was still out in the Philippines, risking their lives looking for the chemical weapons factory that intel said was somewhere out there. And he knew he had the answer locked somewhere in the recesses of his memory.

Or at least he thought he knew it. Or he hoped he did.

He reached blindly across the kitchen for his mug of coffee.

He wasn't a whole man. And only a cruel bastard got involved with a woman like Christy when he couldn't move forward with his life. Not until he resolved this damn dilemma.

Problem was, his dick didn't like thinking about "fair" or "forever." His dick only wanted what it wanted.

Lord, he had better remember what he'd forgotten soon. Otherwise, his next-door schoolteacher was in for one hell of a summer.

OHMYGODOHMYGODOHMYGOD! Christy thought the words over and over as she left the kitchen to relive her mortification in private.

He was so hot! Ripped body, gorgeous tan and blue eyes. He had blue eyes! What angel had smiled on her to give her such an awesome kitchen-mate? No wonder she'd been dreaming about him. She'd probably seen him coming or going sometime yesterday and had constructed a fantasy. Who wouldn't?

Oh, my God, was she still drooling?

And why was it the first time they'd met, she'd had her hair wrapped in a towel and was slurping Froot Loops. God, she had the worst luck ever. She took a deep breath and tried not to feel completely stupid over their encounter. But instead of reliving her humiliation, her mind went straight to *that* moment. It was the one where he'd been close enough to kiss.

He'd just taken the cereal from her suddenly weak wrists and she'd pulled the towel out of the way. And they'd just stood there looking at each other. She hadn't thought about the wet strands of hair plastered against her cheek or that she probably had milk on her chin. She just had the strongest desire to kiss him. It would have been so easy! And he'd been *right there.*

She hated that her mind had gone straight to some very wicked places just because he had an amazing rock-hard body.

So she hadn't given in to her dark fantasy. He was a person, damn it, not her personal sex toy. But wow, she'd give a lot to have a summer fling with him. That was not a politically correct thought, but right now, she didn't care. She'd come to Hawaii to make a change, do new things, and a summer fling was something she'd never, ever done before. All the men she'd dated at home were bland, boring and treated her with kid gloves. A hot marine was as opposite from them as she could get.

Of course, there were a zillion sexy military guys all over this base, but Capt. Jason White was the one she wanted. He was the guy she prayed would fulfill her adolescent dream of a man *out* of his uniform. So long as he wasn't in a relationship—and assuming she was clear that at the end of the summer, she was headed right back to Cincinnati—then there was nothing to stop two consenting adults from steaming up the Pacific island.

That was her plan. She was going to have a fling with her kitchen-mate. She just had to think of the right way to seduce him.

3

CHRISTY WATCHED JASON explode out of the water. He was like Adonis rising from the depths even though it was really the shallow end of the swimming pool. His golden body shed the water in sheets while errant drops clung and sparkled in the sunlight. It was a sight that could have been shot in slow mo and aired on movie screens all over the world. But you couldn't tell that from his face.

No, despite the fact that Christy was only one of several women ogling his taut body and skimpy Speedos, Jason looked furious. It was a tightly controlled anger. He was a marine, after all, and she suspected he rarely lost control. But as he grabbed a towel and collapsed onto a beach chair, Christy felt his frustration as clearly as if it were tattooed across his rippling pecs.

So she did what she always did when she felt someone was in pain. She grabbed a bribe and waded right in.

"Hey," she said.

He looked up and squinted at the bowl in her hand. "Hey," he said.

"I brought this for you. It's my specialty." She tucked her sundress skirt beneath her as she settled into the chair beside him.

He took the bowl from her hand, probably more out of politeness than interest. But his eyes had lightened with humor as he looked back at her. "Ice-cream soup?"

She nodded. "I figured after that workout, you needed the calories way more than I did."

His gaze traveled to the pool and his frown returned. "Yeah. Thanks." He said it as if he meant it, but he set the bowl aside.

"Punishing yourself isn't going to help anything."

His gaze cut to her and there was a coldness there that would have been daunting to anyone who hadn't grown up with two brothers. But she had, so she wasn't fazed when he spoke in a clipped tone. "What did you say?"

She shrugged. "Yes, I know I'm being pushy and a busybody, but after that display, I figured someone had to talk to you before you ended up back in the hospital." She'd done some subtle checking on her kitchen-mate since this morning. She hadn't learned much. Just that he was here recovering from a medical problem. Since he wasn't obviously limping or anything—though some of his scars looked very new—she guessed he was on the tail end of his physical recovery. About the time when the psychological stuff became really brutal.

His stare threatened to become a glower, but he held it back. Again, probably because he was being polite. "What display?" His voice was low and quiet, and it sent shivers down her spine.

She tried to speak gently. "You were attacking the water like a boxer might do to a punching bag, but it was water. And you were mad."

He opened his mouth to say something, but she held up her hand. She already knew he was about to tell her to go to hell. But she had extremely macho brothers, which gave her experience, and a need-to-help heart, which made her super-nosy. She couldn't help it. It was how she was wired. "Summer of change" or not, that part of her personality wasn't going anywhere.

"I know I'm butting in, so let me be short and sweet. My guess is that you're pissed off because you somehow think your body has failed you. Logic doesn't matter. Reason doesn't make a dent. You're a guy and a powerful one at that. Something happened and you realize that you can't will your body into submission. So you're mad and you're punishing yourself—or rather your body—because of it. And again I say to you, that's not going to get you where you want to go." Then she picked up the ice cream and shoved it back into his hands. "So get some sugar into your blood, and then—after you've finished that bowl—you can tell me what I can do with my advice."

He just stared at her. She'd seen the look before. Her brothers or her father would glare just like that when she managed to bully them into submission. She, the one who some days could barely walk, still had the spirit—and the mouth—to corner them. Annoyance was always clear on their faces, but also resignation. And a grudging respect. That was the best part: when her big bad brothers gave her a little respect.

Thankfully Jason was no different. He started to speak, but she quickly pointed to the bowl. So he lifted the spoon and began to eat her ice cream. And since he couldn't talk, she decided to fill the silence with chatter.

She knew from experience that crowing about her victory was a bad choice. So she leaned into her chair and looked out across the crowd at the pool. "I didn't spit in it or anything," she said. "You probably weren't thinking that, but my brothers would be. No, I just shared hot-fudge sundaes with my new student Judy. That's her over there."

She gestured across the pool to a freckle-faced twelve-year-old with strawberry-blond curls and a stick-thin figure. Jason followed the gesture, his eyes narrowing as he took in the girl who was hanging out at the side of a group of preteens. Judy's whole posture screamed *awkward,* especially as she perched a half step back from the group, neither fully engaging nor backing away. Christy's heart broke seeing the girl hovering there, watching life go by without grabbing hold.

"I'm tutoring her in algebra. Not my most favorite subject, but I'm beginning to realize math isn't the real problem." She fell silent, watching as Judy laughed too loud at some joke.

"What is?" Jason's voice didn't startle her as much as abruptly bring her attention back to him.

"What?" she asked.

"What is her problem if it's not math?"

"Oh. Well, what is everyone's problem at twelve? 'How do I fit in? I'm ugly. They think I'm a dork. I am a dork.' You know how it goes."

She glanced over at him, seeing his thoughtful gaze on the girl. He didn't say anything, and Christy noted with approval that he had indeed finished all the ice cream. Then she realized what she'd just said. He wouldn't have been an awkward twelve-year-old. More likely, he'd been the scrappy kid everyone allowed into whatever group simply because no one could ever say no to him.

"Oh," she said out loud. "You probably don't remember an awkward phase. That wouldn't have been your problem."

His gaze cut hard back to her. "And what would have been my problem?"

"Not failing at anything you put your mind to."

His eyebrows arched. "That's a problem?"

She shrugged. "Yeah, it is, the minute you hit an obstacle you can't will your way through."

He snorted. "I'm a marine. I'm used to impossible obstacles."

"Which you overcome. Until you hit the one you can't."

He shrugged, but the gesture appeared forced. "There's always a way through or around something. And if there isn't, you learn how to accept and go on."

She stretched out her legs in front of her. "So how's that going, big guy? The accepting part?"

He didn't answer and in a moment, she wasn't surprised when he turned the conversation to her. Conversational aggression, a patented guy technique to avoid facing more personal issues. "So what are you going to do about Judy?"

She looked at him. "Do? What do you mean, do? I'm going to tutor her in algebra."

"But you said that's not her real problem." He gestured again to where the girl was still half attached to

the group as the others gathered their stuff to go somewhere. Even from here, she could hear the girl thinking: *Do I force myself on them? No one invited me to
join. Am I pushing in where I'm not wanted? I should
just go home. No one wants me here anyway.*

Sure enough the other kids started moving away.
One of the girls hesitated, looking back uncertainly at
Judy. But then one of the boys said something and she
turned away, the invitation unspoken. Judy lifted her
hand in a sad little wave as everyone else moved on.
Then a second later, she swatted at a nearby chair and
shuffled off in the opposite direction.

Heartbreaking.

Christy sighed. Childhood sucked. It shouldn't, but
it usually did.

"Someone needs to talk to the other kids. Get them
to bring her along."

She canted a glance at Jason. "'Cause that's gonna
help. An adult ordering the others to accept her. Any
friendships she makes will always be cast in doubt."

His frown deepened. "So you just leave her to sink
or swim on her own?"

"So I feed her ice-cream sundaes even though I'm
on a diet and I get her to talk about who she is inside.
If I accept her, maybe she'll be strong enough to risk
showing that to someone else too."

He chewed on that for a moment. "That's pretty
deep for a summer tutor." He said it like a compliment,
so she took it as such.

"There are no shortcuts, even in childhood. Especially in childhood. We want to go fix it for her, but all
we can do is give them the space to be who they really
are. The rest falls where it will."

"Voice of experience?"

She laughed. "You asking if my early years in teaching had me telling kids who to accept and how to play? Well, yeah, it did. But I also spent a lot of years watching from the sidelines. I picked up a few things along the way." She smiled. "Mom used to say I was psychic. I knew things about people without being told. Truth is, I'm just really, really observant."

"I'm observant," he said. "You're…a lot more than that."

"Okay, so maybe observant plus experienced." She glanced at his empty bowl. "Feeling better now that you've got some blood sugar?"

He snorted again, obviously about to deny it. But he didn't speak. Instead he gave her a sheepish smile. "Yeah, all right. Maybe things look better after ice cream."

"Always my motto."

"Or maybe it's because I'm sitting next to a gorgeous woman who does not need to be on a diet."

A smooth move if ever there was one. Smooth and obvious, but that didn't stop the zing of excitement deep in her belly. But before she could respond, a quick flash of regret hit his face before he turned away. Like he was sorry for taking the conversation to a sexual level.

"Jason?"

"Hmm? Oh, I was just thinking that I'm feeling restless. It's not good for a marine to be restless. I need to do something."

Now, it was her turn to snort. "So we're back to punishing yourself."

"What?" The word was clipped and hard.

She gestured again at the pool. "Tell me I'm wrong. Tell me that your extra anxiety has nothing to do with a problem you can't solve. Tell me that you're not burning energy out of anger and I'll shut up. But you seem awful pissed off to me."

"I'm not angry!" he snapped. Then he abruptly flushed and moderated his tone. "I mean, yeah, maybe I'm frustrated, but when I'm angry, believe me, you'll know it. Everybody knows it." He lowered his voice and leaned forward a bit. "I'm a yeller. When I get angry, I get right in the asshole's face and just let fly."

"That's not anger. That's a military thing. You call it discipline and whatever. But if I had to guess, you tuck fury deep inside, bury it hard. Then you go blow something up. Don't marines like explosives? Like to an unhealthy degree?"

He didn't answer for a long while. She found she liked that about him. That he didn't blurt out the first thing that came to his mind like she often did. No, he was a thoughtful man. And then, he smiled at her. A slow smile that had her thoughts heading somewhere very different indeed.

"I'm going with your mom," he said. "Definitely psychic."

"Don't I wish. It would make tutoring a zillion times easier. Or maybe not. I'm pretty sure I don't want to know what my fifteen-year-old boys are thinking."

Jason chuckled. "I'm pretty sure you already do know what they're thinking. Especially if you were wearing that dress. And I'm pretty sure it wouldn't be in words. More like graphic—"

"Stop!" she said, laughing. "I really don't want to think about my students in those terms."

"Fair enough!" he said as he abruptly surged to his feet. "Come on. I feel like a bike ride. Wanna join me?"

She smiled up at him. He was holding out his hand, offering to help her up. She took it, almost shyly, not because she was embarrassed about touching him. On the contrary, with the things she was thinking, hands were the smallest of touches she wanted to share with him. It was more about his unexpected offer. A bike ride. When was the last time someone had asked her to go riding?

"I…" she began.

"Do you have another tutoring appointment?"

"No. No, I'm done for the day. But…" But what? She rapidly thought of an excuse. "I don't have a bike."

"That's okay. They rent them along the beach. Come on. It'll be my treat."

She shook her head. "There's no way I can keep up with you. You'll spend the whole time irritated because I'm huffing and puffing behind you."

He frowned. "What am I? Eight? I'm not talking about training."

"Good, because you already did that in the pool."

He shrugged. "I'm talking about a leisurely bike ride. I'll show you the base and stuff."

She hesitated, but only for a moment. After all, wasn't this why she was in Hawaii in the first place? To do things that no one ever asked her to do? To push her limits without someone coddling her? An afternoon bike ride was exactly what she needed to do. She'd be fine if they went slow.

"Okay," she said. "Lead on. I'll follow." Or die trying.

4

WELL, SHE CERTAINLY WASN'T an athlete. Jason smiled as Christy huffed out another breath. They had finally biked their way to the rise on a very small hill. Her cheeks were flushed, her breasts bounced distractingly as she moved, and she was so cute that he was rock hard just from seeing her pant.

"Look at that view," she breathed as she gestured out at the rolling waves of the Pacific.

He was looking at the view he wanted to see, but he forced himself to look away. Especially since he was not in a place right now to start a relationship. Even a temporary one. And definitely not one with a settle-down-and-marry girl like Christy. Still, it was awful hard to bring himself to look at the waves.

"Ooh! I think those are dolphins!" She hopped off her bike. He saw her grimace as she stepped down and wondered if she'd twisted her ankle, but she was walking just fine as she stepped to the edge of the path. The view wasn't all that great. She had to peak through a small break between two buildings and below the waving fronds of some big tree. That, naturally, had him stepping right up behind her to see where she was pointing.

His hands actually itched with the desire to wrap around her waist and pull her against him. She was wearing shorts and a loose tee that could be lifted up with the slightest effort. Her scent spiced the air and just the tiniest tilt of his head would have him nuzzling her neck. But he held himself back.

"Nice," he said, not meaning the dolphins.

She twisted to look back over her shoulder at him. Her eyes were sparkling. "You're not even looking."

"Yes, I am," he answered absolutely deadpan.

She tried to shove him backward. He didn't move. He liked being close to her, even though he'd just told himself to leave her alone. Truthfully, he liked everything he'd discovered about her. Easy on the eyes was only one of her attributes. She laughed a lot. She spoke her mind. And she even had a kid's enjoyment of biking even though she was obviously not used to it. It was as if this whole bike ride was a special treat for her. One that he got to share.

That was sexy as hell, and he had to remind himself to remain a gentleman. Meanwhile, she rolled her eyes.

"You guys are all the same. Never notice the tropical scenery. Just the girl in the bikini."

"Wait," he said with a mock frown. "There's a tropical scene somewhere?"

"The bikini girls are over there," she said, gesturing down at the beach.

His gaze didn't even flicker. "You don't need a bikini to make guys look at you."

He spoke the absolute truth, but she turned away as if embarrassed. It wasn't false modesty, he realized.

She really was uncomfortable with her body's appearance.

"Hey," he said, touching her shoulder. "I was trying to give you a compliment."

She twisted to face him, bit her lip, then said, "You know how you always want what you don't have? Well, I've always wanted to be fit and toned like them." She gestured toward the girls playing beach volleyball. "Instead, I'm soft, round and have a full rack."

He arched his brows at her semicrude term, but it didn't throw him. He liked that she was speaking honestly to him, so he answered in kind. "Guys like full racks."

"That's all guys see. Clothes never fit right, guys assume I'm easy, and people think I'm lazy because of the weight."

He didn't know how to answer that. She was right in part. Her breasts were the first thing people noticed about her. But in a good way, not bad. At least as far as he was concerned. She crossed her arms, distracting him again, which probably made her point.

"You're not fat," he said emphatically.

"Thank you, and I know I work hard to keep it that way. I just wish… I just wish I had a different body, that's all."

He frowned, a little disappointed in her. She seemed like such a confident woman, it surprised him that she had issues with her appearance. He'd known scores of women who obsessed endlessly about ridiculous "flaws" in their appearance. Your body was your body. There were lots of ways to get it healthier, but wishing to be taller, chestier or whatever was a waste of time.

She was moving back to her bike, slipping around

him as best as she could. Moving completely on impulse, he held out his arm to block her path.

"I could help you get more fit," he offered. "Simple exercises to improve your cardio, light weights. Nothing—"

"Nothing like what a marine does before breakfast?"

He flashed a rueful smile. "No one expects you to be a marine. But if you want to be more fit, then do it. An hour a day—"

"Will keep the doctor away. Maybe for you, but I'm civilian all the way. I'll never be able to keep up."

She moved around him to get back to her bike, and this time he let her. She walked stiffly while he just stood there and watched her, pieces slowly fitting into place. "Your father was military, right?"

"Air force. Why?"

"And did you have brothers?"

"Two. Air force and navy, respectively."

"So you were the only girl?"

"Yeah. The youngest of three."

Now he began to understand. "That must have sucked growing up. No way a younger girl can keep up with two older brothers. Physically it just can't happen. So why bother?"

She studied him, obviously thinking. He liked that she was listening to him, actively processing his words instead of merely reacting. In the end she released a heavy sigh. "You know why I teach kindergarten?"

He shook his head. Truthfully, he hadn't known what grade she taught in Ohio.

"Because the kids don't let me tank out. Any other grade, you can sit at a desk at least part of the time.

You can rest a bit, take a load off, do something less physically demanding."

"Not in kindergarten, huh?"

She scoffed. "The last time I took a five-minute break, Joey stuffed a Barbie shoe into his nose."

"Ouch."

"Yeah. You'd think he wouldn't have pushed something that pointy up there, but he did."

"And you learned to never sit again."

"Oh, I do. After school. But for eight hours a day—I teach both shifts—I'm moving all the time. Because the kids demand it."

He frowned, working to sort through her message. "Are you trying to say that you work hard enough?"

"No. I'm saying that without someone forcing me, I don't work at all. A little cardio would be good for me. I can try an hour a day."

"I'm not forcing you," he said. "You have to—"

"I want to," she interrupted. "You're not forcing anything on me at all." Then she eyed the path, looking both ahead and behind. "So you think you can find a way back that will take an hour? A *light* hour."

He smiled. "Yes, ma'am, I can."

In truth, the journey took an hour and fifteen, and at the end of it, he could tell she was wiped. By the time they made it to her room door, he could tell they'd overdone it. Her gait was very stiff, but she was also smiling, clearly happy. And he had never felt so relaxed either. They'd managed to talk for almost the entire ride. He used it to gauge her exertion level, but honestly, it had been awesome to swap childhood stories.

She'd grown up on base with older brothers who found ways to run wild. He'd grown up on the poor side of Indianapolis where running wild was the only way to survive. There was a lot in common between them, yet also enough of a difference to make the telling exciting. But now that the time was over, he found himself looking down into her eyes and wanting something so much more from her than shared stories.

"This was great. I had a great time," she said.

"Yeah," he said, looking at her lips. "Um, hey, make sure to pop some ibuprofen. Don't want you sore tomorrow."

An expression flashed across her face that he couldn't read. Humor? Regret? Annoyance? He really had no idea and the second it registered, it disappeared. Then it occurred to him that she might not have any pills. It probably wasn't the lifesaving staple that it was for marines.

"You know, I have a whole bottle—"

"I got some. Don't worry. I'll medicate."

And then they both just stood there, her with her back to her door, him leaning over her about half a breath away from kissing her.

"You were right," he said abruptly.

She blinked. "About what?"

"Earlier. When you said I was mad about something. About how my body has betrayed me somehow." He slumped against the wall, knowing he needed to confess this now or he'd never get it out. "I was in a jeep and we drove over an IED."

She gasped. "An IED like a *bomb* IED?"

He nodded. "Yeah. We were lucky that it was really badly made. Five of us, and we all got out alive."

He saw the shudder run through her whole body, and remembered why he didn't talk about these things with civilians. It was horrible, but it was also something marines learned to deal with from day one. They could get blown up any minute. If you were lucky, you survived. Nobody liked it, but you either dealt with it or went nuts.

"I'm fine, obviously. Weak, out of shape, but coming back."

"You're not weak, Jason. You're a moron if you think you're weak."

He dipped his chin. "Okay, I'm weaker than I used to be. But like I said, my strength's coming back. But there's a different problem."

She watched him closely, clearly waiting for him to continue without pushing him to speak before he was ready. It took him a breath, but he got there.

"I've got amnesia. I can't remember stuff before or after getting blown up."

"I'd think that was normal. And that you probably won't get everything back."

He nodded. "That's what the docs say."

He'd gone over it a thousand times in his head. The mission had been to find a biological weapons factory. They knew it was somewhere in the Philippines. That's it. *Somewhere* in a whole freaking country. But using logic—and a lot of footwork—they'd found it. Or rather, Jason had found it. He'd figured out where the thing was right before getting blown up by the IED. And now he couldn't remember where it was.

His unit continued on, doing what they'd been doing. Logic, intel, on-foot searching, the whole nine yards, but they weren't getting anywhere. Jason could fix it all. He had the answer. It was just locked up tight in his brain, hanging there behind a big wall of nothing. He couldn't even begin to express how frustrated and angry that made him.

Meanwhile Christy touched his chest. She put her fingers right on his sternum, and it was like getting touched by a branding iron. He felt every one of her fingertips. Not painfully hot, but just there. Like he would remember her fingers on his chest until the day he died.

"So what's the problem?" she asked gently.

"There's something important that I have to remember. That's the one thing I *do* remember—telling my best friend that I knew where it was. See, our mission was to find something. And Danny said I'd just figured it out when it happened."

"When you drove over the IED?"

"Yeah." He swallowed and looked down at the floor wishing for the zillionth time that he could break through the damn wall in his brain. "I knew something. I knew where it was. I'm sure of it."

"But you can't remember?"

He shook his head. "Nothing. Nothing at all."

"So you're pissed."

"Yeah." She'd summed it up perfectly. He was angry about getting blown up. Angry that he couldn't remember. Angry that it was right there, but he couldn't grab hold of it. "My guys are still searching. They're still risking their lives because I can't think of where the damn thing is. And I'm…here."

"Healing," she said firmly. "You're here healing. You have to do that before you can remember."

He banged his head against the wall, then stopped when he saw her wince. "I know," he said, forcing himself to keep his tone level. "I know, but I'm impatient."

"There's a shocker…not."

He smiled at her wry tone. "The thing is," he said slowly, without looking at her, "I'm messed up right now. I'm angry and frustrated and in therapy, which really is no fun at all." He heard her chuckle at that but didn't move. "And the minute I *do* remember, I'm out of here. I'm going to have to go back to my unit and help them. That's my job."

"Okay," she said. "Why are you telling me this?"

He opened his eyes and went for brutal honesty. "Because I want to kiss you right now, but I can't. First off, I'm not me. Not the normal me."

"You're changing. That's not abnormal, it's just different."

"Different is still not the time to start things with a girl."

She grimaced, but he didn't let her comment.

"And besides," he rushed on, "I'm leaving at any time. The second I remember, I'm gone. No warning, no nothing. I'll just be gone."

"I grew up on base. I know about here today and gone tomorrow."

He reached out and stroked her cheek. God, she was so pretty. Her eyes were huge, her skin soft, and her lips were right there. What he wouldn't give to sink right into them. Into her.

"I'm not going to do that to you. Or to me. I don't want to be thinking about you when I should be focused on my men. On whatever it is I need to remember—"

"I get it." She'd interrupted him, her voice low, but she repeated it louder when he stopped talking. "I get it. I don't like it, but I've learned that when a marine gets stubborn, there's nothing I can do to change his mind."

He frowned, startled by a sudden surge of jealousy. "You spend much time with marines?"

She laughed, the sound light, and it warmed him despite the fact that he was putting the brakes on their relationship. "Let's just say that in some ways, there's little difference between a stubborn marine, a stubborn air force officer and a stubborn six-year-old. You're not going to listen to me. All I can hope is that you'll catch a clue and come knocking on my door sometime soon." Then her eyes met his. "No strings attached."

His breath caught. She was offering him a fling. A no-strings-attached hot—

She kissed him. She had to go up on her toes to do it, but one second she was looking at him and the next her mouth was pressed up to his. And she was doing something with her tongue that shorted out his brain.

A split second later, he wrapped his arms around her and drew her tight. Her mouth opened beneath his, and he went straight in. He heard a soft sound, a womanly sound that was half delight, half surrender, and his blood fired hot. He pressed her against her door and owned her mouth like he was staking a claim.

It went on for much too long. Or not long enough. He adored the feel of her, soft in the right places and solid in the rest. She kissed like a dream, and he was finally skimming his hands underneath her shirt when a noise in the hallway alerted him.

It was nothing really. Some kids were playing outside. One of them laughed, loud and raucous. But he was a marine and trained to pay attention to outside noises. To realize that he was about to strip her naked in a public hallway. And to know that this was a bad idea even though every cell in his body was pushing him to take the two steps into her bedroom and do what they both wanted.

So he broke the kiss, dropped his forehead against hers and just breathed. Breathed in, breathed out. And waited for the lust to fade.

It took a really long time.

"I've lost you, haven't I?" she said, her breath curling about his neck and kicking his pulse into overdrive.

"It's too fast," he said. "I can't think."

She laughed, though the sound was forced. "I never thought I'd be the one trying to convince a guy to have a summer fling with me."

His body tightened against her despite his intention to pull away. She gasped and his blood roared. But he was a man, damn it, not an animal. He was not a slave to his lusts, and he would not walk down a road that he knew was wrong. Despite her words of a summer fling, she would fall deep and hard. She was just that kind of girl. And, truthfully, he was that kind of guy.

"I don't have summer flings," he said. "I don't have a girl in every port and I don't seduce women just because it will fccl so damn good."

She touched his face, her fingers gentle and her question honest. "Why not?"

"Because when I go for a woman, I go for keeps. I proposed to my high school girlfriend and when I caught her with someone else I joined the navy. I've dated other women, but they weren't right and I knew it."

She let out a little moue of regret. "So you already know I'm not the right one."

"I don't know any damn thing!" he snapped, his frustration making his hands fist against the wall. "I only know that I can't remember and that I have to and you're a distraction."

"Sometimes a distraction is a good thing. Ever think you're trying too hard?"

"Every damn day. But I can't *not* think about it either." He forced himself to step away from her. It was hard, but he did it. "I'm messed up, Christy. Which means that this is not the time for me to do anything with a woman. It's not fair to either of us."

She nodded. The gesture was slow and filled with an embarrassed kind of pain. He'd rejected her and that had to sting. But he knew she understood. He wasn't rejecting her, he was rejecting the situation. Romance was not a complication he could afford right now.

"Maybe after I remember… After I figure out—"

She held up a hand. "Don't make it worse, Jason. You're not ready for anything more. I get it." She sighed. "And you're probably right. I don't know that I'm good at flings either."

It bothered him that she was even thinking of a summer fling. It bothered him in a Neanderthal kind of possessive way, and he ruthlessly pushed that thought aside. Meanwhile, she opened her room door.

"I think I'm going to take a shower now. Maybe a bath too."

He didn't understand what that meant, but didn't comment on it. "Good idea. I might do the same." Though the idea that they would both be wet and naked some few feet away from each other was not going to help their situation.

"I still had a great time today, Jason."

"Yeah, me too."

She looked like she wanted to say more, but in the end, she gave him a little wave and stepped into her room. He stood there watching the door close, feeling like a rejected suitor—and the irony of that wasn't lost on him. Then he shoved his hands into his shorts and headed for his own shower: a cold one.

It worked for a while. He managed to *not* think about her for at least two or three seconds. He grabbed some dinner and ate it morosely, all the time wondering what she was eating and what she would think of the soggy fries or the bad O-Club decor. And when he wandered back to his room that evening, he looked at the stars and remembered how she had been so excited at seeing the dolphins.

And then he went to bed and dreamed about her.

5

CHRISTY WAS DREAMING. She knew she was dreaming because she felt no pain. She was walking through the base on her way to the swimming pool and her knees didn't creak, there was no persistent ache in her hips, and even her spine felt like it was fresh and new.

She took a deep breath, loving the feel of such easy movement. And as she exhaled, she saw him: Jason. Adonis rising from the depths of the swimming pool, his body all sleek and golden. She saw his scars with new understanding now. She recognized the anger that haunted his expression and added a clipped edge to his gestures. She knew the source now, and her heart ached for him.

But this was a sunlit dream, and there was no time for pain here. So when a child ran past her chasing a Frisbee, she laughed at his antics. He tripped over something, but he scrambled to his feet and ran on. If she wanted too, she could run after him. She could run and play as she'd never been able to as a child. There was no pain here. Except, of course, Jason's pain.

She turned away from the children. She was interested in more adult entertainment anyway. So she took Jason's hand and together they walked. They ended up on the beach, the people and the background melting away as they can in dreams. She didn't care. All that mattered was the man beside her.

"I understand your choice," she said. "You were probably right to stop us before."

"Christy," he said, the word half worship, half desperate longing.

She touched her fingers to his lips. "This is a dream, Jason. And here, I can do what I wanted to before. Here, I can give you some little release because you won't let me in real life."

"I wanted to. I wanted you," he said against her fingers.

"Shh," she whispered as she pulled her hand back so she could kiss his mouth. "Let me do this. Because I really want to."

She stroked her tongue across his lips. He opened for her and they played together like that for a bit. His arms wrapped around her and she gloried in his strength. But soon, she wanted more and so she broke from his arms.

"Don't move," she said. "Not even a little bit."

He tilted his head, his brows arched in surprise.

"My dream. My rules." Then she grinned at him. "Parade rest, soldier."

"I'm a marine, Christy."

"Oh, right. Parade rest, sailor."

"Aye-aye," he answered. Then he widened his stance and locked his hands behind his back. She stepped back a bit to admire him. His broad shoulders, his golden skin over washboard abs, and his wonderful erection. Clothing was strictly forbidden in her dream.

Now she could kiss him at her leisure, wherever and however she wanted to. His mouth, his chiseled chin, and his neck were first. But she quickly went lower, glorying in the ripples of his chest, the tight bud of his nipples, and the way his heart thundered beneath her lips.

He tasted like sunshine and strength to her. Like every stroke of her tongue brought forth sparks of bright light that tingled in her mouth. And when she swallowed, she brought his lightness into herself, letting it warm her body and electrify her blood.

The strength came from her, though. Because in this dream, her joints were normal and movement was easy. She could do as she willed with him, without fear of spending days in aching stillness on her bed. And better yet, as she used her most powerful body, she could bring this god of a man to quivering lust. She could make him weak with hunger until he collapsed at her feet.

At least that was her plan, and so she set about doing it with leisurely skill.

She kissed down his belly, nipped at the tattooed bird on his hip, and then inhaled deeply of his musk as she finally got to stroke his erection. She was on her knees now before him, but it was a ridiculously easy position to hold. One glance up at his face told her his breath was coming in ragged pants and his eyes were burning for her.

"Christy—" he began, but she shook her head.

"Not a word, not a move, Jason. Not until you collapse at my feet."

"But you don't have to—"

"I do," she said.

He took a deep breath, his chest expanding. And then as he exhaled, she felt his buttocks tighten and his body ready itself for her. Then just before she took him in her mouth, he said something that stopped her cold.

"You don't have to do it clothed, do you? You can give me a peek, can't you? Even if I can't touch."

She blinked, startled that he would ask such a thing in her dream. Her attention had been on what she was about to do, not on how she looked. But he'd made her think of it, and so she complied. Better yet, since this was a dream, she could perform acrobatic feats that would be impossible in real life.

"Very well," she said. Then she rose up before him. She was dressed in her usual yellow sundress. Nothing fancy, but this one had a zipper in back. It was a simple matter to reach behind and slowly pull down the zipper. And then she let the dress drop off her shoulders to pool at her feet. Even in dreams, she wore a full support bra and panties. Though this set was made of black lace that stood out against her stark white skin.

"You have the most gorgeous body," he breathed. "Great breasts, and your waist is perfect. And turn around. Please turn around. I've been staring at your ass for two days now and all you've worn are skirts or loose shorts. Let me see it for real."

She straightened, surprised by his words. Had he really been looking at her butt? Really?

She stood before him, slowly stretching her arms above her head. She watched his eyes flow over her breasts and he licked his lips. Slowly she turned around, but twisted enough to see his face. Damn, his eyes definitely dropped to her bottom.

"Permission to touch?" he asked.

She grinned. It was thrilling to have a man look at something other than her oversize breasts. "Granted, sailor."

His hands found her bottom immediately. And though he'd gotten to her fast, his caress was anything but. He stroked slowly over her hips before cupping her ass. Just to see how he'd react, she slowly bent over.

He groaned, and the sound seemed to travel straight from the depths of him, enough to make her arch.

"Christy," he whispered, and she felt him step forward.

She leaped away because here she could do that without wincing. "Back into position, sailor!" she cried.

He froze, and the look on his face was comical. "But—"

"My dream. My rules."

He frowned at her and returned to parade rest. But he seemed downright confused as he shook his head. "I must have a really twisted subconscious."

She smiled and returned to facing him. "You mean my subconscious, sweetie." She popped her bra and pulled it away. His eyes practically bugged out of his head. "And why wouldn't I want to dominate a ripped marine?" She hooked her thumbs under the straps of her thong and shimmied it down.

His penis twitched as she moved. She knew he was holding himself back, but his gaze all but burned her wherever it touched. And it did touch her everywhere.

"I take it back," he said. "My subconscious knows exactly what I like."

"Really?" she said as she teased him. "Does it like this?" She lifted her breasts, one in each hand. She began to knead them, pretending to get herself really hot. Except, of course, it wasn't pretend. Especially as she widened her legs and began to stroke herself. She'd never done that in front of a man. Couldn't even imagine doing it anywhere except for right here. Right in front of a man who could overpower her in a second, but chose—by her command—to keep himself absolutely still.

She didn't come. That wasn't what this dream was about. And though she was definitely worked up, she wanted to touch him. So she eventually returned to her knees in front of him.

She stroked his penis, loving the velvet feel of his skin, the thick pulse she imagined in her hand, and the wet slide of moisture at his tip. She could see the sunshine where she touched him. A light that seemed to come from inside him, but flowed hot and hungry into her. It was desire, she realized. Hot, wicked hunger for her. And maybe some love, too. There was some emotion there that went beyond sex. She was sure of it even if she didn't examine it too closely. Whatever it was, she wanted more, and so she bent her head and took him in.

She played with him then, however she wanted. Stroking his penis with her tongue, caressing his ass with her hands. Soon, his body was shaking. She knew he was close and she wanted it all. Right now. Sunshine and desire, all mixed together in this dream, and she demanded every iota of what he had to give.

She felt him erupt.

Bliss!

She drank it all and felt filled with light.

CHRISTY WOKE with a cry that quickly changed into a gasp of pain. After such lightness of heart and body, it was a cruel trick to dump her back into her real body. She tried to move, feeling how stiff every joint was, and wincing as both knees crackled.

She glanced at her wristwatch. Barely 2:00 a.m. She grabbed the glass of water and pills she'd left on the nightstand and swallowed them as fast as possible. She was pushing the dosage. She'd hoped to sleep through until morning. But she hadn't, and no way could she last until morning awake. So she took the pills and lay like a corpse in her bed. Sometimes, if she didn't move at all, the pain eased enough for her to sleep.

Or other times—and apparently this was one of them—the pressure to move built up and she knew she'd have to go for option two. It was a ridiculous thing to do. She knew that. Her father hated it and her mother usually hid in the bedroom when she did it. But every doctor she'd spoken to about it had shrugged and encouraged her to pursue whatever worked. She had tried to wait it out. Sometimes that worked. But not tonight. She was too keyed up after the day—and the dream—spent with Jason.

So, option two. She supported herself and managed to get out of bed, stabilizing her swollen feet beneath her, and hobbled as carefully as she could to the bathroom. She tried not to bend too much as she walked, keeping her knees to a very easy angle and her spine stiff with almost no rotation. It wasn't so much the bright flashes of pain. Those happened intermittently, and she'd long since learned to accept them. It was the gnawing ache of every step, every breath, every movement.

Her joints were swollen and they didn't want to move. Predictably, the worst was in her knees. After all the biking, she knew that might happen. But there was pain in her ankles, which led to swollen feet and the like. If she let it continue, the ache would tighten up her shoulders which would lead to a raging headache. Option two was designed to head that off at the pass.

She made it to the bathroom and plugged the tub. She ran the cold water then hobbled her way to the kitchen. She'd already made the ice just in case. It was the first thing she did when coming to a new place, and so she had plenty of ice cubes stored up.

It took a few minutes, but soon she was dumping the ice bucket into the water and waiting while the tub finished filling. And then, her ice bath was ready.

She stripped out of her nightgown, tossing it aside. Then she stretched herself across the tub, lifting a leg, poising herself for the drop. It was always best to submerge fast. Inch by inch never worked.

She took a few deep breaths, the pressure to act building in her mind. There was something that clicked deep inside her when it finally reached a certain level. Pain, pressure or just neuroses, it didn't matter. It was time.

She dropped herself into the ice water.

She gasped, her mind going white in shock. Her entire body seemed to seize up, drawing tight to her spine. Even her breath shrunk to nothing as her diaphragm froze.

Cold. Mind-numbing cold rolled into her consciousness. As if her whole body were lost to one long scream of agony. But if she waited long enough the scream faded. It grew distant, like a train whistle shrinking into the background. And with it went all sensation. What remained was silence. And blessed numbness. She felt nothing but the lingering impression of pain somewhere so removed from her blanked mind as to be completely unimportant.

Silent.

Cold.

Done.

CHRISTY BLINKED BACK to awareness, realizing that her teeth were chattering and her fingertips were blue. She didn't have a clock nearby, but she knew it had probably been ten minutes or less since she submerged. Either way, it was time to get out.

The lower half of her body was numb—which was the point—so she had to maneuver with weak and trembling arms. At home she had special railings installed so she could drag herself out safely. But this was temporary quarters on base. She could still manage it, but it was harder than she thought. Her legs were heavy and barely responsive and the sides of the tub were slick. She managed to haul herself out, but when her right foot was supposed to take her weight, it didn't. She half slid, half fell, her arms going every which way and the—

Ow! Her head impacted hard with the toilet and she cried out. Then she was on the floor, still stunned, one arm pinned beneath her, and a throbbing just behind her eye.

Ow. Ow. Ow.

She lay on the floor panting, annoyed that all the work of having a pain-free lower half had just been destroyed by a throbbing headache. And now sensation was returning to her lower body. Hell.

Then she heard it. Jason calling her name. Had he been banging on the door? She didn't know.

"Christy!"

Definitely Jason. She tried to call back, tell him she was fine. Her voice came out as a croak. And then it was too late.

The door crashed open and he was there, his face going white as a sheet as he looked at her: naked, bloody, and half sprawled on the floor of the bathroom.

Shit.

6

JASON HAD JOLTED AWAKE at the culmination of the best wet dream ever. It was about Christy, of course, making him stand at parade rest while she did what every soldier fantasized about at some point during every parade. It had been heaven, and he'd woken in a release like he hadn't experienced since he was thirteen.

He'd cleaned up and then had just lain in bed trying to sort through his thoughts. About Christy. About the damn thing he couldn't remember. About life in general and his future.

Then he'd heard Christy bumping around the kitchen. Heard her get something out of the refrigerator and then leave. They were homey noises, and he listened harder, liking the idea of someone nearby. He'd had his thirtieth birthday and he'd like to start a family. He'd always wanted to be a father, and the settled life with a wife and kids was abruptly appealing in a way that had never grabbed him before.

He'd let his mind drift, imagining himself and Christy married, maybe with a child on the way or better yet, a toddler with her dark hair or his blue eyes. He'd felt a yearning that stunned him. A longing for the life and the woman that couldn't possibly be real. But it sure had felt real.

And then he'd heard the thump and a cry. Muffled but clear enough. No chance that he'd imagined it, so he was out the door and through their shared kitchenette before he'd fully opened his eyes.

The kitchenette door was locked. He'd banged on it and called her name, but hadn't heard a response. He was just wondering if he'd imagined it when he heard her voice. A thick croak that could have been a cry for help.

No question now. It had taken one well-placed kick for him to be through the door. Then he was in the dark bedroom and to the bathroom in less than a breath. Only to stop short at the sight of Christy bloodied and on the floor.

"Don't move," he ordered as he did a scan of her body. Bloody forehead, swelling bruise. Obviously she'd fallen while getting out of the bathtub. Not that serious. What worried him were her blue lips and the awkward way she was resting on the ground. Impinged nerve? Spinal damage?

He knelt beside her, careful of his footing on the wet floor. She was trying to straighten up and reach for a towel, but he put a hand on her sternum to keep her still.

Cold. Bloody hell, she was like an ice cube.

Though the panic clamored in his throat, he gently helped her pull her arm out from under her but steadfastly refused to let her up.

"I'm going to call for an ambulance. I want you to—"

"I'm fine, Jason." Her voice was rusty but clearing rapidly. "I just slipped."

"Happens all the time," he agreed with a smile he knew probably looked strained. "Just stay there. It's best if we—"

"I'm fine!" she said with clear anger. Then she shoved him backward with a grunt—or tried to—before pulling herself up into a sitting position. Her legs barely moved. They looked like deadweight to him, and that worried him even more. But he was reassured by the strength in her shove. Not that it had him going anywhere.

He dropped his hand to her leg and tried not to flinch. Ice-cold again. Colder even than her chest. This was not good.

"Stop staring," she said as she grabbed a towel and flung it over herself. "And while you're at it, back up so I can get dressed."

He shook his head. "You're going to stay right there until the ambulance—"

"You are *not* calling an *ambulance!* Jeez, Jason, I slipped! It happens."

He took a deep breath, keeping his eyes steady on hers as he tried to calm them both. "Something's wrong with your legs, Christy. I'm sure it's nothing, but your skin is really cold right now—"

"Happens with an ice bath."

"It's probably nothing, but…" It took him a moment to process her words. "Did you say 'ice bath'?"

In answer, she gestured to the still-full tub. He looked, then had to look again. There were ice cubes floating in there. He carefully dipped his fingers in, quickly pulling them out.

"You were in there? On purpose?"

She snorted, her eyes starting to sparkle with humor at his stunned tone. "I fell *out* of the tub, not into it."

"But…but…why?" As a marine, he'd been forced into cold water too many times to count. Pool water, ocean water, arctic water. All sorts of waters, but none of them at home because he thought it'd be a good time.

She touched his face, drawing his gaze back to her. "I'm not nuts, Jason. I'll explain it all to you in a second, but you have to back out of the bathroom. Sitting naked on a tile floor is really not my idea of a good time."

He nodded. What she said made sense. But no way in hell was he letting her stand on her own. Hell, she'd just hit her head if nothing else. So he simply slipped his arms underneath her and lifted.

She gasped and threw her arms around him. He held her tightly, trying not to wince at the very cold temperature of her skin. Instead, he tucked her against him and willed her body to warm. All he had on were loose boxers so he had a lot of body heat to share. If it weren't for the wet towel between them…

He cursed and grabbed the thin thing and pulled it away. She probably didn't want to be naked in front of him, but too bad. She was cold, damn it, and she shouldn't be. He quickly carried her to her bed.

He was being protective. He was trying to be a good friend. But he was also a guy, and his body had the predictable reaction as he cradled a naked woman to his chest. He was concerned for her, damn it. But hell, she was beautiful and lush and—as incredible as it sounded—having her in his arms felt better than what they'd been doing in his dream because this was real. She was real. And he wanted her.

Her eyes were wide as he cradled her, her mouth only a couple inches away. He was looking at her, and she was staring back. And both of them were thinking things they shouldn't. He could see it in her eyes.

But she was hurt. And still cold. And he really ought to get some pants on.

"Don't move," he ordered as he quickly set her down then covered her legs with the blanket. She started adjusting the pillow behind her back, but he took over the task as soon as she started to move. "Are you sure you didn't hurt your back at all?"

She huffed as she pulled the blanket up to cover her breasts. "I'm sure I only hit my head. But I'm about to hit yours if you don't chill."

He told himself it was appropriate for her to cover herself, but part of his body mourned the loss of the view. To console himself—and because he was still rattled—he slid his hand under the blanket to touch her shin. Jeez, she was still ice-cold, but warming.

"I'll get a towel for your hair."

"Thanks," she said with a resigned sigh.

He turned to go, but not before seeing an array of pill bottles on her bedside table. His eyes narrowed as he counted. Three bottles, all prescription. Hell.

"Do you need…" He gestured lamely at the bottles. "I can get you a glass of water."

"I already took what I needed before the bath."

"Okay." He crossed to the bathroom and grabbed

the only remaining dry towel. Hair dryer too, which he unplugged with a little more force than necessary.

He returned to her, gave her the towel, then immediately worked to plug in the dryer. She towel-dried her hair, then silently took the hair dryer from him. She made quick work of it while he kept his eyes on her lips.

Not blue anymore. That was reassuring. The glare she shot him was not.

"Jason, you've got to relax. Honestly, you're worse than my mother."

He winced at that, then turned away to pull up a chair. He would not risk sitting on the bed with her. It was too easy for him to get distracted, even worried as he was. So he sat nearby and waited while she finished with her hair.

Eventually, she set the hair dryer aside, tugged the blanket back up almost to her neck, and leaned back against her pillow to glare at him. "I'm dry. I'm warm. Anything else you need?"

"Want a cold compress for your eye? You're going to have quite the shiner."

She gingerly explored her eye. She'd long since wiped away the blood from the cut on her forehead.

"I'll be fine. I *am* fine. I just overdid it this afternoon, that's all."

He arched his brow. She had to know he wasn't leaving without a full explanation.

She sighed. "My joints swell. There are lots of different doctor words attached to it, but it's really just arthritis. I've had it since I was little. It's worst in my hips and knees, but all my joints are…sensitive. They really swell when I do too much."

"Like go on an hour-long bike ride?"

She grimaced at the anger in his tone. "Yeah. Like that."

"Hell, Christy, why didn't you tell me? I was pushing you! If I'd known—"

"You'd treat me like a fragile flower the way everyone else who's ever known me does. That was part of the reason I took this summer job. To be someplace where nobody knew."

He leaned back in his very hard chair while the pieces fell into place. She'd kept repeating that she couldn't keep up with him. Or her brothers. She wished she had a different body. She'd talked about how she liked working with kids because they forced her to move. How otherwise she'd just sit and not do anything. Maybe perhaps because it hurt for her to move.

He rubbed a hand over his face. "You should have told me."

"I thought I could do it. We didn't bike for long, and I haven't been doing anything since I got here. Tutoring algebra is nothing like crawling around with kindergarteners. I thought I could do it."

"So what happened? How bad does it hurt?"

"It's an ache that spikes when I move my legs."

"And an ice bath helps?" He could hardly believe it. That seemed like smashing your foot with a mallet because you stubbed your toe. Sure the toe didn't really hurt anymore, but your entire foot was in agony.

"I know it doesn't make much sense. The first time I did it was on a dare from my older brother. I couldn't compete running or wrestling or anything like that. But stupid tolerance games? Oh, yeah, I could take as much if not more pain than they could." She lifted her chin. "Very idiotic, but damn if they didn't respect me more afterward."

He snorted. "Kids do love to be stupid." But he could see the need in her to challenge herself. Even in something so crazy as pain tolerance.

"It's hard to explain," she said. "But once I sub-merge—"

"You submerge?" He gasped.

"Not my head! Just from the waist down. But there's this whiteout of pain that obliterates everything else. And then it sort of recedes—"

"Fades out. Sure," he said, knowing what she meant. Every marine made a study of pain and unique ways to make it disappear. "I get it. But how bad is it now? If you had to go to an ice bath to numb it, then it must have been—"

"It was…uncomfortable. It's fine now." She was lying. He could tell. But he also knew she had too much pride to complain about a pain she'd been dealing with her entire life. So he nodded.

"Fine. But, uh, mind if I sit with you for a bit? I'm a little too shaky to go back to my room."

She laughed, her eyes alight with real humor. "You are such a bad liar."

"Am not!" Hell, he was going to be haunted by the sight of her naked and bleeding for the rest of his life. He never, ever wanted to see that again. "Promise me that the next time you decide to make yourself a pop-sicle, you call me. I'll help you out of the tub."

"Won't that be hard to do when I'm in Ohio? Or if you're...wherever you're going?"

"Yeah, it will. So I guess you'll just have to hold off on becoming Ms. Freeze for a while."

She shook her head. "No problem. I think my exercise days are over."

He could have let that go. After all, she had a real medical problem and he was certainly not trained in how to handle that. Shouldn't he let her and her doctor work out the details of an exercise plan?

But he couldn't forget how she'd talked about wanting a different body. One that was more fit. One that could handle the stresses of her usual day with more ease. And he was damn sure that a stronger cardio system and a little more muscle tone would ease some of the pressure on her joints. Plus, she obviously hated it when people babied her. That all added up to one thing.

"Hell no, you're not stopping the exercise. Like you said, you just overdid it today."

She frowned at him. "I don't think I'm up for any more trail rides."

"Thank God, because it's really expensive to rent those bikes." It was a lie designed to make her smile. It succeeded, which gave him the opening he wanted. "So instead of biking, you're going to swim with me."

"Ugh," she grimaced. "Me and a bathing suit haven't gotten along since I hit puberty."

Now there was an interesting thought. His dick twitched with interest.

"But you have one, right?" he pressed.

She nodded reluctantly. "My friend forced it on me when she heard I was coming to Hawaii."

"Good friend. Smart friend. Swimming is easy on the joints and good conditioning. If your legs hurt too much, you don't even have to use them. Just let them dangle while your arms do the work."

She groaned. "Now I know you're a marine. The answer to every problem is to work out."

"Not true," he said with mock outrage. "Solution one is to blow it up. Solution two is to work out."

She folded her arms and gave him the evil eye. He almost laughed.

"You'll have to do more than give me a dirty look to get me to change my mind."

"I thought we weren't going to have a relationship. I thought you were too messed up in the head to have time for me."

He grimaced. Yeah, obviously the no-relationship bit wasn't working out how he'd planned. After that wet dream, he sure as hell knew his subconscious wasn't going to let her go. And after seeing her on the bathroom floor, he was always going to worry about her. Add to that his fantasies of her as his wife and mother of his children...well, the no-relationship thing didn't seem like such a good idea anymore.

Still, he made one last attempt at doing the right thing. "Being someone's workout coach is not the same as being in a relationship."

She stared at him, her expression shifting from a glare into a thoughtful chagrin. "I don't know, Jason," she said. "You charged into my bathroom to rescue me then carried me to my bed. You brought me my blow dryer and now you're going to oversee my athletic health. A girl could get used to that kind of attention. And maybe even a little more, if only for a few days."

"A girl could, huh?" he asked.

She nodded.

"Well," he said as he pushed out of his chair to join her on the bed, "so could a guy." And then he kissed her.

7

CHRISTY ACHED, and not in a painful way. True, it was embarrassing to be caught tumbling headfirst out of an ice bath. But the way he'd come to her rescue and lifted her right off the floor. Well, that put him in her hero category for sure. Add to it his being a marine, gorgeous, and clad in nothing but his shorts, and she was hot in a way that no ice bath could cool.

Just based on that, she would have wanted to go to bed with him. She *did* want to go to bed with him. But he was also kind and funny. And…and he was Jason, her next-door neighbor who was kissing her with lips that clung and teased. She sank into him. She closed her eyes and let everything in her submerge into him.

He penetrated her mouth, his tongue gently stroking. He didn't need to be so careful of her, but she could not get him to hurry. He took his time pushing into her mouth and withdrawing. Push, withdraw. While his hands caressed her jaw and neck.

"Touch me everywhere, Jason. You don't have to be careful. I can handle it."

He pulled back, his eyes searching her face. "Maybe

you can, but I don't know about me. Do you know I've been dreaming about you? I can hardly believe this is real."

She flushed, remembering exactly what she'd been dreaming about doing to him. She'd love a repeat, only in real life, but honestly didn't know if her back and legs would take the pressure. It didn't matter because he was pressing her into the bed.

"I dreamed something really hot with you," he said as he braced his arms on either side of her. "It was awesome, but now I want to reciprocate."

She giggled. He made her giddy and nervous all at once. "You don't have to—"

"Just lie back. It hurts to move, right? With swollen joints?"

"It's the weight more than the movement. Pressure on the knees. Pressure on the hips. I'd do better if I lost some weight, but that's not easy."

He shook his head. "You don't need to lose an ounce. And as for pressure, just lie back. Let me do this for you."

"But—"

He silenced her with a kiss. It was a great kiss, warming her blood until every part of her hummed with delight. When she started to say something, he pressed a finger to her lips.

"Not a word, Christy. But you're allowed to moan." He flashed her a smile. "Or you can scream my name."

She arched a brow. "Really? Is that a challenge?"

"We marines like a challenge. Game on?"

She laughed. Only Jason would make sex a competition. A really fun competition. So she nodded. "Game on." Then she sealed her mouth tight as if she would never open it again.

"Perfect." Then he touched his mouth to hers again. Nothing aggressive. And he didn't even try to slip his tongue between her lips. Just a simple press, then a lick of his tongue, before he began to brush long strokes of his mouth against her cheek and jaw.

Never had she thought a man's mouth could be so exquisitely gentle. Or so erotic. She felt his breath heating her skin, the ultrasoft caress of his lips, and the occasional rasp of his teeth along her jaw. His fingers danced below her chin, and she let her head drop back with a sigh of delight. He was like a pianist playing her neck, and it was both ticklish and erotic.

Then he pulled the blanket down. She knew it was coming. Especially when his mouth left hers to begin a trail of kisses along her body. But he didn't pull the blanket down quickly. In fact, he wasn't doing anything quickly and it was both torturous and wonderful. He inched the covers off her slowly, letting them slip away so she felt the movement on her now very sensitive breasts.

She thought he would touch her then a lot more intimately, but he sat back and looked at her instead, his eyes dark and intense.

"Damn, Christy, you have the most gorgeous breasts."

She flushed and knew that her skin had gone rosy.

"You into just watching, sailor?" she asked.

If she thought that would push him into action, she was utterly wrong. He just grinned at her.

"With you, Christy, I think I'm into it all."

He waited a bit longer, watching her while her nipples tightened. Wow, how had he done that? Gotten her hot with just a single long, appreciative look? Then he finally began to touch. Both hands. Softly caressing. Then he slid under her breasts and lifted them slightly, groaning in delight.

"I thought you were supposed to make me moan," she quipped, impatient.

"You have no idea how I've fantasized about this."

"Really?"

"Really."

To prove it, he rolled his thumbs over her nipples and she gasped in surprise. She didn't know if it was the anticipation or the way his large hands fit her breasts perfectly. Whatever it was, she shivered, relishing each sensation. He was shaping her breasts, playing with them and tweaking her nipples, while her body tightened and grew restless with hunger.

God, he was good at that. And from his grin, he was enjoying it as much as she was. Then he canted a mischievous look at her.

"Time to start that moaning, Christy."

She shook her head. "Not unless you make me."

He did. He bent his head to her nipple and sucked it into his mouth. Lightning shot through her body straight to her womb. She arched slightly off the bed, and her eyes drifted closed. And as he began to stroke her nipple, she gripped his shoulders and moaned. God, that felt great.

And when he switched to the other nipple, she was in heaven. But apparently it was a restless kind of heaven because she wanted more. She wanted him between her legs, thrusting into her.

"Jason…" she cried. She ran her hands down his back and tugged at his shorts. "Get undressed!"

He lifted his head. "That wasn't a scream."

"Not happening from what you're doing now." She worked her fingers under his shorts and tried to push them down. But she didn't have the angle, especially as he slid lower on her body, his hands leaving her breasts to press down on her pelvis, keeping her still.

"You're moving too much Christy. And my weight—"

"Will be just perfect on top of me. Jason, don't make me beg."

He grinned. "That's a different game. Tonight we're playing Scream." And then he slid his fingers between her legs.

She almost sat bolt upright. Truthfully, it had been a long time since a man had touched her there. Most guys didn't seem to know what they were doing. It always seemed to be a half fumble kind of thing. Not a problem with Jason. She didn't know if it was a marine thing or just him, but he was confident as he began to stroke her.

Oh, lord, he *definitely* knew what he was doing. His fingers were long and calloused as they opened her right up. They stroked and penetrated, causing her to gasp as his actions built the fever in her blood. Her belly tightened. Her skin took on that flashpoint of heat once. Twice.

Oh, yes.

And then he started to lick her. She'd barely even noticed him shift position, but she felt his tongue now. What his fingers had been doing was magical. What his tongue did sent her right over the edge.

"Yes!" Her body contracted, arching and shivering in pleasure. Climaxing was lovely, the wave delight-

ful. But it ended too soon. As she regained her breath, she looked down at his grinning face.

"Good?" he asked.

"Yup," she said, her voice coming out more breathless than she intended. "But I didn't scream your name."

He flashed a rueful grimace. "Maybe next time."

She grabbed hold of his arms to pull him up, but he was too large a man for her to do that easily. Fortunately, he moved forward as she collapsed backward. Damn, she felt good, but she wasn't about to let him off the hook yet.

"If you want me screaming your name, you're going to have to use a more manly implement than your tongue." She slid her hand right over his impressive erection.

Yup, even through the barrier of some very old cotton shorts, she could tell he was thick and hot and very hard.

He gasped when she gripped him, but then he grabbed her wrist to stop her. "I don't have any condoms."

She jerked her head to the bedside table. "Top drawer. It was a have-a-great-summer gift from a friend."

He leaned forward and pulled out a brand-new economy-size package from the drawer. He arched his brow. "Now that's a friend."

"She said I couldn't come back unless I'd used every single one. She was the only one who thought coming out here was a good idea."

"Hmm," he said as he ripped open the box. "There's a lot of summertime fun in here."

"I guess we better get started." Then she stretched

up, catching his face so she could kiss him full and deep, before he stood up. Without breaking the kiss, she pushed his shorts off as far as she could. He had a great butt, and his muscles tightened beneath her fingers.

She heard the condom wrapper rip. Impressive that he could roll it on without looking and still keep kissing her. But then he was a marine, and they were skilled at all sorts of unique and special things.

She smiled in reaction to her thoughts, and he lifted his head. "You're not supposed to be laughing."

She ran her hands over his bottom then squeezed him just like he had been doing to her breasts a little while ago. "I'm appreciating, soldier."

"Sailor."

She giggled. "Whatever. I believe I have an SOS—"

She gasped as he spread her legs and settled onto his knees between her. Then he slid his very big hands right under her bottom and lifted her up, leaning forward over her.

She watched what he was doing as he positioned himself. It was amazing seeing his corded thighs, his jutting erection, and her spread wide before him. She'd never gone in for erotic pictures, but this sight was one she'd never forget.

She raised her gaze, sliding over washboard abs, golden pecs, and then up to his face as he watched her.

"Christy?"

"You're gorgeous, Jason. I can't believe—"

He thrust into her. One deep push, and he was inside her. Thick. Huge. And so startling that she screamed, "Jason!"

He froze, deeply embedded in her. "Was that a good scream or a bad one?"

She caught her breath, feeling him so big, so there inside her. "A good one," she gasped. "A great one!" Then she gripped his shoulders and arched to better accommodate him. "Do it again."

He moved slowly, withdrawing inch by very long inch. She raised her knees and let her head drop back.

He slipped into her again and again, landing deeply every time.

The tension was building once more, her blood already hot from before.

"And again?" he asked, humor lacing his tone.

"You're killing me here. You know that, right?"

"Say my name again and you'll get your wish."

She opened her eyes, meeting his dark blue gaze. "Jason. Now."

He did as she'd asked and she cried out at the impact.

"My name," he said as he pulled out again.

"Jason."

Another thrust. Powerful and deep. Oh, God, she was close.

"Jason."

She was gripping his hips with her legs, making this one count.

"Ja-son."

"Jason!"

8

BEEP-BEEP! BEEP-BEEP!

Christy turned off her alarm clock without even opening her eyes. What she did do was spoon back against Jason with a murmur of appreciation. He was wrapped around her, their legs entwined.

"What time is it?" he murmured as he drew her closer.

"Too early," she answered.

He pushed against her backside, nuzzled at her neck. "Are you sure?" His hands were traveling to her breasts and he was fitting himself...

God, yes. He was perfect. And she was happy to wake up in the best way possible.

Until he froze. "Oh, shit, Christy, is this okay? Are you hurting?"

It took her a moment to understand he was referring to her joints. "As long as I'm distracted by you, Jason, I don't feel anything else."

"But—"

"And you're the one who's going to be hurting if you don't finish what you started."

He paused and then placed a long, wet kiss at the base of her neck. She shivered. God, she loved it when a man licked her there. "Yes, ma'am."

And he proceeded to distract her thoroughly.

Sadly, it couldn't last forever. The snooze alarm went off and she was forced to face the day. One that didn't involve lounging around in bed with a handsome marine.

She pressed a swift kiss to his cheek. He'd collapsed sideways with a very male grin on his face, his mouth pressed into the mattress.

"I gotta shower," she said.

He mumbled something unintelligible, and she smiled. Then she rushed through her morning routing while trying her best not to slip into fabulous daydreams that relived the night before.

By the time she was stepping out of the bathroom, he was on his feet and heading her way naked. He was a beautiful man, even with morning beard and bed head. She stood to the side, taking some time to look him over. Broad shoulders, narrow waist and the sweetest...

Her breath caught. She stared. She let her eyes drop to his corded thighs, then raise up again over clear tan lines. It was still there, right on his hip where she knew she'd never seen it before.

A tattoo of a bird that looked almost like a swallow. Just like she'd seen before...*in her dreams.*

She closed her eyes a minute, blocking out the distracting sight of him while she tried to remember. When could she have seen that before?

Not last night. They had certainly touched each other everywhere last night, but in the dark. She hadn't actually *seen* his bottom much less the little tattoo on his hip. So how had she known it was there? How had she *dreamed* it?

"Christy? Everything okay?"

She blinked and forced herself to focus. "I'm fine. I'm, uh… Don't laugh. I'm just freaked out because of your tattoo."

He frowned and looked down at his hip. "The swallow? My mom had a thing for birds. Used to draw them and stuff. After she died, I got drunk one night, took one of her drawings and…" He gestured down. "You're a military kid. You've got to have seen tats before."

She nodded. "Scores. The thing is…" She giggled nervously. "Well, I dreamed that tattoo when I dreamed about you and me on a beach. And even before, in an earlier dream. I…uh, well, I dreamed it."

He leaned against the wall, his eyes taking on a heavy-lidded sensuality that was half seductive and half male preening. "So you were dreaming about me…"

"Don't get smug," she said as she crossed to the kitchenette to grab some coffee. Thankfully, she'd programmed the coffeemaker last night. "You're hot. I'm a healthy young woman. It's not surprising that I did nasty things to you on a beach in my dreams." She lifted her mug and took a heavenly first sip. "And before you go all cocky on me, I dreamed about you giving me a facial too."

He had been prowling over to her, probably more to steal some coffee than to seduce her. He was still naked, and she was still a little freaked about that tattoo. But she was in no way prepared for the way his whole body jerked to a stop.

"I was…uh, I was giving you a facial?"

She smirked. Her manly marine didn't like the not-so-manly implications of that. "Yeah. It was this little room. I could hear kids laughing outside, and you were mixing—"

"A bowl of mud. And it wasn't a facial. It was a full-body rub."

She frowned, trying to process what he was saying. "Yeah, it was a full-body scrub. And I saw your tattoo on your hip. I remember because I thought it was unusual and cool at the same time."

"And there were kids laughing outside but you said to pay attention to you." He leaned against the counter as if bracing himself. His eyes were wide, but probably no larger than her own. Goose bumps rose on her arms.

"Christy, when did you have this dream?"

"Second night here. The day before we met in the kitchen."

He nodded slowly. "Me, too. Same night."

She frowned. "Same dream? Are you sure?"

"I don't usually dream about giving a woman a facial. Yeah, I'm sure."

She straightened. She couldn't possibly be thinking what she was thinking. I mean sure her family called her psychic, but they were joking. She couldn't read minds. Her dreams and his dreams…they couldn't be *sharing* them! Could they?

Then her thoughts skipped to the *other* dream she'd had of him. "Oh, my God. The beach dream."

He met her gaze, his expression as horrified as she felt. "Last night?" he said, his voice a near whisper.

She nodded. "I, um, I—"

"Best damn dream of my life." He bit his lip, his cheeks coloring a ruddy red. "Did you dream you, um—"

"On my knees. You were at parade rest—"

"Parade rest."

They said the words at the exact same moment.

He paled. She felt dizzy. "It's not possible," she murmured.

"Completely ridiculous," he agreed.

She bit her lip. "On the beach. When did you see me?"

He frowned, obviously trying to remember. "I was coming out of the swimming pool."

"Uh-huh," she said. "We started at the pool."

"There was this kid—"

"Chasing a Frisbee. He tripped—"

"And you took my hand and said it was a dream."

"I said it was a dream and that I wanted to give you…"

"A release." He flashed her a sheepish grin. "You did. It was amazing."

"That's when I saw your tattoo. And the other time too, when you were mixing the facial stuff. You had your back turned to me and I saw it."

He took a deep breath. "This is really weird."

She didn't know what to think, so she looked away. And she saw the time.

"Damn. I'm late."

He blinked. "Yeah. You need to go. And I need to… think."

"I…" She what? She'd gone down on him in a dream and then he'd done the same to her in real life? She just couldn't process it. It was too bizarre. And yet…

"It's not a big deal. So we're dreaming things." He didn't sound like he believed his own words.

"Great things," she said with a flush of embarrassment.

"It's okay. It's not weird at all."

Of course it was weird. But it wasn't necessarily bad, right? She bit her lip. "I've really got to—"

"Go." He grabbed her arm just as she started to leave. "Have dinner with me tonight. We can...talk."

"Okay. Great. We'll talk."

"Tonight. Meet here at six?"

"Six it is."

Then they stared at each other for another long awkward moment. In the end, he pushed her toward her open room door. "Go."

So she did.

JASON SAT DOWN hard on his bed. The shower hadn't helped. Two mugs of coffee hadn't helped. He should go for a run or something. Maybe that would sort things out.

It was a lie. He knew nothing would sort *this* out, and yet really, what was the big deal? So he and Christy had had dreams about each other. They were right in the middle of the fun sex-all-the-time part of their relationship. Of course they'd dream about each other.

But the same dream? The *exact* same dream? That wasn't possible. But then again, it kind of explained why he had a dream about being a spa guy. A *naked* spa guy. That was obviously Christy's contribution to the experience.

He grinned when he thought about that, choosing to focus on the fact that she thought he was hot. That she'd thought he was hot before they'd even officially met. That was cool. But…

This wasn't getting him anywhere! Yeah, he was full on in lust for the woman, even if it wasn't for the dreams. That part was already loud and clear. As was the part about Christy being a distraction. After all, he was supposed to be remembering that location he'd forgotten, and he'd just spent his morning thinking about Christy and her—their—shared dreams.

Holy hell. He needed a run.

He ran. He swam. He saw his therapist to whom he said absolutely nothing at all about his dreams. He was freaked out, but he wasn't stupid. Talking about shared dreams would be career suicide, especially in the military. They did, however, talk about Christy and some of the things he'd done with her in the real world.

In the end, Jason agreed with the doc: women were good. Sex was good. He should stop trying so hard to figure things out and just enjoy both.

Which worked out great until he met her for dinner.

9

THE FIRST THING that he noticed about Christy was that she was gorgeous. No big surprise there; nor was the slam of lust that hit him deep in his gut. He knew she wore sundresses because they were light and easy, but they also looked amazing, highlighting her tight waist, those bombshell breasts, and legs that were curvy, just the right length and bare. They made his hands itch for wanting to stroke up them.

"Hi, handsome," she said as she opened up the door to him. He wasn't wearing anything fancy. Black jeans, casual button shirt, all solid colors. He was a solid-color kind of guy which, according to his sister, was *boring*. But Christy didn't seem to mind as her eyes sparkled up at him. And, best of all, she even wet her lips.

He took the invitation, even if it wasn't one. He leaned down and kissed her. It was meant to be short and sweet, but she had some flavored lipstick on and, damn, he just liked kissing her. Short became deep, sweet became hot. And a second later, he had her pressed against the wall.

He pulled back, trying to catch his breath. "Sorry," he said, his voice a rasp. "I asked you out to dinner, not another grope fest."

"I like grope fests," she quipped. But when he looked into her eyes, she held up her hand. "But I'm really hungry. Think I can take a rain check?"

"Definitely."

She grinned and he almost forgot he was being a gentleman. She had the most lovely grin. It lit up her whole body. He had the feeling that even her toes smiled. That was a marked contrast to himself. He was always in the wait-and-see camp. Wait and see if what he feels is real. Wait and see if someone's in it for the long haul. Wait and see if what he thinks he remembers is what really happened.

Wait and see, which meant he took her hand in his and led her out to his waiting car.

"I, um, I thought we'd go out to dinner off base. I know this really good seafood place. The decor is kinda tacky, but the food is great."

"I love seafood. It's all I've been eating since I got here. Well, that plus the fruit."

He nodded and held open the car door for her. She didn't need him too, but he liked going old school, especially with a woman like Christy. She deserved all the gentlemanly manners he could muster. She flashed him her wonderful smile as she settled into her seat.

And then the happy interlude ended. The moment he got into the car and started driving, she started talking about things he'd wanted to forget.

"So, I had a little time this afternoon. I spent it doing research into shared dreaming. There's a lot of stuff out there. I mean *a lot*. All sorts of theories on how and why it happens. No real rhyme or reason as far as I could tell…"

She spun off into one crazy theory after another. Obviously she'd put a lot of time into this. He tried not to listen. In fact, the way his heart was thudding in his ears, he couldn't really hear more than one out of every three words. And then she stopped and stared at him.

"Jason?"

"Hmm?"

"You're being awful quiet over there."

"I'm driving."

"Uh-huh. Do you seriously think I'm going to buy that?"

He glanced at her. He should have known she wouldn't fall for his typical line of BS. She was a teacher, after all. No one could spot crap as fast as a good teacher.

So he shrugged. "Look, we don't really know that… Well, that you and I…" He couldn't even say the words aloud. Naturally, she had no problem with it.

"Are sharing erotic dreams?"

He swallowed. "Uh, yeah. The thing is, guys have, um, dreams like that all the time. There's nothing unusual about that."

"Dream you're an esthetician often, do you?"

He frowned. "A what?"

"A guy in a spa who puts seaweed mud on women."

"Oh. Yeah. No. That was a new one."

"Well, that's an oldie for me, but a goodie." She twisted to face him more fully. "But I never dreamed anyone I knew doing it to me. Or that he was naked and with a tattoo I'd never seen before."

Watch the road. Watch the road. Jason focused

nearly exclusively on the yellow lines, doing his best to block out Christy's words. He was a guy and a marine. Things like this just didn't compute in his world.

"I get it," she finally said with a sigh. "You're not buying it. It's pretty out there."

"It's pretty damn impossible."

"And yet, you were naked in a spa applying the seaweed."

He made a sound that was almost a growl, but he strangled it. He was not frustrated with her. He was *not.* He just didn't like the idea of being part of something supernatural. Whereas she, obviously, was getting off on it.

"They're just dreams, Jason," she said gently. He almost glared at her.

"They're my dreams. And they're private!"

She swallowed, and he immediately cursed himself for being a jerk.

"I didn't mean that the way it sounded," he said.

She nodded slowly. "Okay. So how did you mean it?"

He turned his attention back to the road and belatedly realized he had the wheel in a death grip. So he consciously relaxed his hands and spoke as rationally as possible. "I just don't like someone else having access to my brain, is all."

"Even me?" Her voice was soft. "Are you afraid that I'm going to kill you in your dream or something?"

His stomach sank straight into his boots. Hell. He hadn't thought about that at all. But now that he did… "Jeez, Christy. It's more likely the other way around. I mean, I'm a marine. What if I think you're the enemy and shoot you?"

"Well, I guess I have to believe that even while dreaming you can tell a good guy from a bad one."

Obviously she hadn't shared dreams with a *marine* before. Everyone had friendly-fire nightmares. Friendly fire, unfriendly fire, random acts of terrorism. The idea that she would be caught up in one of *those* dreams was flat-out terrifying.

"Aren't we getting a little ahead of ourselves?" she asked. "I mean, the kind of dreams we're sharing don't exactly involve guns or anything."

Okay, that was true. And good news. And there was nothing inherently wrong with having hot dream sex. Especially since they were having real sex now.

"Wait a sec," he said. "You're right. We've been having *erotic* dreams."

"That's what I was saying—"

"Which were born of sexual frustration, right? I want you, you want me. We say no in the hallway then..."

"Parade rest in our sleep."

He grinned. Hell, he'd never be able to stand at ease again without remembering that dream. Quite the perk, in his opinion. "Yeah," he said. "But see, we're not frustrated anymore, are we?" He glanced at her and saw that she had flushed a little. "So long as we go to sleep satisfied..."

"You don't think this will happen again?"

He was counting on it. Meanwhile, she sighed. "Okay, so you don't want to do it again."

He waggled his eyebrows at her. "Hell, yes, I do."

She snorted. "Not that. You don't want to explore the dream state again."

"I think it was a fluke, whatever it was."

She didn't answer at first, and he was very afraid that she would push the point. But in the end, she just said, "Fine. I think it's cool, but obviously you don't."

"Don't make this into a big deal, Christy. Please."

"Fine. I understand. Not everyone wants to dive headlong into something this weird."

"I find reality challenging enough."

"What if we fall asleep tonight and find ourselves on another moonlit beach?"

He shook his head. "We won't."

"But if we do?"

"We *won't*. But if we do, feel free to make me stand at attention as much as you like."

She laughed, which was the exact reaction he'd hoped for. "Okay, we won't talk about this again, but if I show up tonight carrying whips or chains—"

"I will happily tie you down and have my wicked way with you."

She snorted. "As if. In my dreams I'm a fierce warrior woman."

"Of course you are. Good thing I'm always a god in mine. Trumps *Xena, Warrior Princess* every time."

She stretched her legs out in front of her, and he noticed she winced as she moved, although her tone was light. "You're on, soldier boy. We'll see who's got the studlier dream body. I'll take you down."

"Sailor," he corrected. "And when I go down—"

"Oh, stop!" she blurted, knowing full well where he'd been heading.

They were laughing by the time they made it to the restaurant.

DINNER WAS GREAT. Christy ate her fill of wonderful seafood. Better yet, Jason was excellent company. They talked about anything and everything, so long as it was solidly in the *not*-paranormal category. Which was fine. Movies, books, obnoxious parents, funny friends. He loved shoot-'em-up action stories. She loved sweet family dramas. No big surprise there. But they both adored *Dr. Who* and had a lot to say about comic books.

They went to his bedroom this time, and when he finally entered her, she knew there would be no sexually frustrated dreams tonight. He made her wait forever for her release, but when it came, she was surprised she didn't die from the explosiveness of it all. She never thought sex could be that incredibly good, but with him it was. In part because she never knew what was going to happen. He could be playful one moment, then incredibly intense the next. He watched her closely, reading her body better than she did. So he knew just where, when and how to touch her.

And God, she loved every second of it. Of him. Of their time together.

She knew she was falling fast. It wouldn't take many more nights like this for her to be head over heels in love with him. She knew it was temporary. He'd made that very clear. Didn't seem to make any difference at all to her heart. She was giving him everything.

So when the dream state hit, one in which he was right there walking down a dirt road, she wasted no time in skipping up to walk right beside him. She wasn't going to waste one single second with her marine man. Real or dream, she wanted them to be together. Even if this time, he wasn't naked.

This time he was carrying a gun and pointing it directly at her.

10

"CHRISTY, WHAT THE F—" He strangled his language and whipped his gun away from her. Then he turned towards the path, his eyes scanning the surrounding area.

She looked with him. It was some dirt track in... Asia somewhere? That's all she could guess from the landscape and people's features. Or was it the Philippines? Whatever. She didn't care. She was more interested in twirling a happy circle right in front of him.

She was wearing her bright yellow sundress again. Today it matched her mood: light and sunny. And she was pain-free. God, she hoped these dreams never ended.

"Christy, you have to get out of here. It's not safe."

She spun around to walk backward, so she could talk to him. "Look, I know this is some marine scary soldier thing for you—"

"Sailor!"

She giggled. "Hey, it's a dream. And that whole dying during a dream thing—I think it's only dangerous if you don't know you're in a dream. But I do. 'Cause we are."

He didn't seem to care. "Stay down!" He grabbed her arm and whipped her behind him. He wasn't exactly in battle-stalking mode, but he was definitely nervous. And he was being protective of her, which was really kinda sweet.

She tapped his shoulder. "Jason, this is a dream!"

He grabbed her wrist and locked her arm behind her back as he hauled her against him. Now this was more like it. Except, of course, that it wasn't remotely sexual. Whatever subconscious state he was in, this wasn't a shared erotic dream. At least not for him.

"Listen to me, Christy," he said in a hushed voice. "You don't belong here. You have got to leave. Now."

He was angry and frightened, she realized, his tension vibrating straight into her. Obviously, this dream wasn't going to go like the others. Disappointment filtered through her, but she understood. So she nodded and waited patiently until he loosened his grip on her and she was able to breathe again. Man, he was strong. A moment later he let her step away from him, but he kept his voice low and intense.

"You need to leave. Now."

She gave it a halfhearted try. Nope. Apparently, she couldn't will herself out of this dream either. She looked at him, shrugging her shoulders. "I don't seem to be going anywhere."

He growled at her, then she noticed noise in the background of the dream. It was kids laughing, actually, as they played some sort of rock toss game. She'd been listening to those sounds nearly every day since she became a teacher, but Jason obviously wasn't prepared for it. He spun around on his heel, his gun lifted at the ready.

"It's okay, Jason. It's just some kids."

He nodded, but the tension in his entire body ratcheted up to an unbearable degree. "I know that," he ground out. "But any minute now I'm going to get blown to hell and I don't want you here for that!"

She stopped to look at him more fully. "So you know this is a dream?"

"It's a memory, Christy, now *get the hell out!*"

A memory. Of when he'd been injured. Oh, God. She looked around, trying to see the source of the threat. She didn't see anything unusual. Just a village. A school.

But then the scene shifted. The world became a jeep, rolling down a road. She had time to hear Jason yell at the guy sitting next to him, "Wait! I know where it is!" Then he looked straight at her and cursed. He was just saying her name when the world exploded.

JASON CAME AWAKE with a gasp. Pain rippled through his abdomen where he'd taken shrapnel, but it was mostly phantom pain. His body was nearly healed, the nightmare already fading. But the panic was real.

Christy had been with him. Christy had died!

He tried to see her in his bed, but it was too dark. He slammed on the bedside light, then twisted to find her. Her eyes were open, her breath coming in light pants, but her gaze shifted right to him.

"Wow," she whispered. "I've never been blown up before. Not even in a dream." Then she levered herself up on her elbows. "Are you all right?"

He exhaled, his entire body going limp. She was all right. Or at least, she was alive.

"Jason?"

"I've been blown up before," he said, trying for a light tone. "For real and in a dream. So this is old hat for me."

"Not sure I like your hat," she said as she touched his forehead. She was smoothing aside his hair, what he had of it. Mostly she was just touching him, and he was beyond grateful for the caress.

"Christy," he pleaded. "You can't do that. You can't come into my dream like that."

"I'm not controlling it, Jason. It just happens."

He looked up. "You could have been hurt."

She laughed, the sound only a bit strained. "I got blown up. Just like you. And yet, here I am. I'm fine. Better than you, I think."

She was right. He was the one who was sweating, his heart still pounding in his ears. Not her. No, she was sitting there, trying to smile at him. Like his own personal ray of sunshine in the middle of a very dark dream.

God, how he wanted her. It was a hunger of both body and soul. She eased the darkness in his heart. Just looking at her made his belly unclench and the terror in his mind start to fade. She was a miracle made just for him, and he wanted her to the point of pain. So he took her hand and pressed a long, desperate kiss into her palm. He tried to express in that one gesture how much he needed her.

She reached for him with her other hand, but he held her off. And then he forced himself to set her aside.

"This can't continue," he said, his words flat.

She sighed. "They're just dreams, Jason. I know you don't like that I'm sharing them with you. But who knows, maybe it's a good thing? Maybe I can help?"

"Maybe it's *classified*."

She blinked. He could tell she hadn't thought about that. But now that he'd said it, he saw the implications flow across her face. She was from a military family. She knew better than most exactly what that word meant.

"I didn't see anything. Just a village somewhere."

He groaned. Jesus, that was bad enough. A village somewhere when he'd been on a classified mission searching for something that could get them all killed. "Shit."

"No!" she cried. "It's nothing! I didn't see—"

"I'm a marine, Christy. Most of what I do is classified." He ran his hand over his face, his mind cataloging the many ways he was screwed. "I can't even be talking to you about this."

"It's not your fault! I didn't see anything!"

He closed his eyes. "I'm a security risk now." Hell. His military career was over. Yes, he was leaping to the most dramatic, awful conclusion, but that's what the military mind did. It's not that he thought Christy was selling secrets to terrorists or anything, just that for whatever reason, he could no longer trust himself. He could dream about secret U.S. military bases, classified documents or the details of any mission he'd been on. Details that were highly sensitive. She wouldn't understand a lot of it, but what if something slipped out? What if she accidentally said something to the wrong someone? It wasn't unheard of. Unlikely, sure, but the military dealt with unlikely all the time.

He groaned and dropped his head into his hands. How could this be? He never thought his *dreams* would be a security risk. But that's the way his CO would see it. That for whatever bizarre reason, he was no longer a secure asset.

She shifted onto her knees. "We'll tell your CO. We can explain things." To her credit, her voice sounded doubtful even as she said the words. She knew how ridiculous they sounded.

"Even if they believed us—"

She sighed. She already knew no one would believe this. Hell, *he* didn't believe it and he was living it.

"It doesn't matter," he said dully. "You're seeing things you shouldn't."

"I can keep a secret. I'm a military brat, remember? You don't think wives and girlfriends know stuff they shouldn't?"

She didn't know, she didn't understand. Yeah, it was inevitable that wives knew about classified stuff, but only the little things. Nothing at the level he'd been working. Nothing like his nightmare. Hell, he didn't even want her knowing about this stuff. To see it live? Played out in Technicolor? He shuddered. This was so many layers of screwed.

What if she saw a different mission? Any of his last five were so secret even the smallest details could get people killed. He had to do things as a marine, see things, execute orders that were beyond sensitive. Reporters were known to cozy up to military wives and girlfriends for the accidental drop of stuff just like that. If she said the wrong thing to the wrong person, a PR nightmare would be the least of their problems.

"We have to end it," he said. He was looking down at the sheet, watching as his hands clenched into fists. "We have to stop seeing each other."

"You're breaking up with me? Because of a *dream?*"

He lifted his gaze to her, wondering if she could see how agonizing this decision was for him. He wanted her. Hell, he might even *need* her. But they couldn't keep doing this. They just couldn't. He was a mess inside and out. To add the idea that she was in his *head* was just too much for him to handle. Security risk, bizarre paranormal crap, it didn't matter. He didn't want her that close.

"If you see my dreams, if you *remember* them." He shook his head. "You can't, Christy. It's just…you can't."

He watched her swallow, her face white. "Okay, I'll stop. I won't do it again."

He straightened. "You did this on *purpose?* I thought you said you couldn't control it!"

"I can't! I mean, I thought it was cool. I know you didn't like it, but I thought it was amazing. And you know, what we did in the dreams, it was—"

"Yeah, it was fun. But Christy, tonight was a hell of a lot different than you and me on a beach."

She nodded. "I know. I know. Everything I read about this on the internet said that you have to want to do it. You have to choose."

"I didn't."

"Maybe not consciously. But I did. Each dream, each time, I knew it was a dream and I waded right in."

She touched his hand, but he flinched away. He knew she hadn't meant to betray him, but that's what it felt like. As if she'd chosen to invade his dreams and his privacy. It didn't get more private than dreams.

"I won't do it again, Jason. I…I can fight it. I think I can, at least."

He looked away. "How could you do this? How could you just…do that?"

"I didn't know what was happening at first. I didn't know these were *shared* dreams."

He turned to stare at her. "You did tonight."

She nodded. "But I didn't *know*. And I sure as hell didn't know that I'd be tromping around wherever we were."

Oh, God. "Forget where we were."

"I don't know where we were!"

He didn't answer. Just glared at the sheets and his clenched fists. He was excruciatingly aware of her sitting up beside him. Of the way her breath shifted between angry huffs and frustrated sighs.

"So you're just going to lock me out," she said, her voice raw. "We hit a snag, and that's it. We're done."

He glared at her. "This is a little more than a snag, Christy. This is treason." Okay, perhaps that was overstating it, but looked at objectively, he was sharing ultraclassified information with a civilian. That was treason…more or less.

She rolled her eyes. "It was a dream! And before you start throwing blame around, don't forget that it takes two to dream. I couldn't step in if you didn't want me there."

He grimaced. Of course he *wanted* her there. Jeez, who didn't want a beautiful woman in a place like that? Who didn't want that bright wash of yellow sundress in the middle of a nightmare. He *wanted* her there, but she couldn't be there.

He pushed out of bed, not bothering to answer her. He didn't know what he wanted to say, so he took the coward's way out and headed for the bathroom. He heard her sigh and drop back against the headboard.

He took his time, hoping he'd find a solution. Nothing hit. Nothing helped. It all boiled down to one thing: she was seeing classified information straight out of his head. The whys and wherefores didn't matter. She was seeing things she shouldn't, and he had to stop that. Immediately.

His brain had been betraying him enough lately—with the amnesia and all—he sure wasn't going to let it screw him over more. Rational? Not really. But it didn't matter. He could not let her in like this. He had no control. And it scared him way too much.

He came out of the bathroom and took a long look at her. He absorbed the essence of her, or tried to. Her glorious chestnut hair. Those big brown eyes that just melted his heart. A man could get lost in a woman like her. A man could count himself lucky to marry a woman like her.

He thought those things, saw them all, and then he forced himself to turn away.

"What are you doing?" she asked.

"I'm going running."

"You mean you're running away."

He shrugged. Yeah, that's exactly what he meant, but he wasn't going to acknowledge it aloud.

"There's got to be another choice," she said. "Unless…" Her voice choked a bit, and he turned back to her.

"Unless?"

"Unless you're tired of me already. Unless this is an excuse to end things."

"We never should have begun."

She lifted her chin. "Tired old song, Jason. Want to try for a different refrain?"

He shook his head. "I can't have you in my head, Christy. It's too messed up in there."

She shifted onto her knees. He could see the need in her eyes. And the hope. "I can help, Jason. I swear to you, I can help."

He thought about not saying it. He thought about lying to her, but he couldn't get the words out. So he opted for the truth. "You do help. You have helped. But Christy, I told you before. This was temporary. And I can't—"

"And you can't have me in your head. Because it's classified up there. I know. I heard." She pushed out of bed, grabbing her clothes with jerky movements. He wasn't sure, but he guessed she was holding back tears.

He almost broke right then. Her rigid back. Her stiffness. It all said that he had hurt her and, damn, that was the very last thing he wanted.

"I'm sorry," he said. It was all he could get out.

She nodded, but with her back to him. "Yeah. Me too."

She finished pulling on her clothes. It was the middle of the night, but he knew neither of them was going to get any more sleep tonight. She went toward the kitchenette that would lead to her own quarters. He was close enough to touch her, but he didn't. If he did, he'd break for sure.

He didn't think she'd stop. He was praying she wouldn't stop, but she did, obviously fighting herself even as she turned to look back at him.

"What are you going to do if this doesn't work?"

He frowned. "What do you mean?"

"We shared dreams before we even met, Jason. What if it still happens even without the...the relationship?"

He swallowed, fear churning in his gut. He ran through possibilities in his brain, rushing through them until he landed on the most obvious one.

"I'll sleep when you're working. Stay up all night. If we're never asleep together, we can't share dreams."

"Yeah," she said dully. "That'll do it." Then she shook her head. "But while you're off torturing yourself, turning your nights and days around and the like, I want you to think about one thing."

He arched a brow at her. His throat was too clogged to ask what.

"It takes two, Jason. You had to pull me into your dream as much as I had to go. So there's something you need to share, something you need to work out. And apparently you can't do that alone."

He swallowed. "That's what navy therapists are for."

"Then I suggest you start talking to him."

"Her."

She shrugged, though the movement was tight. "Whatever." Then she turned and walked away.

11

CHRISTY POKED AT her dessert, uninterested in even her cheer-me-up slice of cheesecake. She was sitting inside a base café, one that overlooked the pool. Right out the window, she watched Jason pummeling the water as he swam laps. He was working with the kind of determination only a marine could muster, and a part of her was impressed. Over the past two weeks she'd heard him get up just as she was returning from dinner. Then he'd begin a fitness routine that would cripple most people, but for him, it seemed to be working.

The man was a lean, mean machine. She'd noticed a considerable strengthening in his muscles. His chest had bulked up, his ass had tightened up—not that it was all that loose before—and every part of him was ripped. He could have been a cover model.

She'd noticed because she'd watched. Turns out even on a base as large as this one, she could manage to catch glimpses of him everywhere. They never looked at each other directly, though she guessed that he was seeing her every bit as much as she was obsessed with him. She'd caught him looking at her a few times, especially when she was out with her students. She liked tutoring outside in the sunshine. It seemed to help everyone.

But every once in a while, an itch between her shoulder blades would have her looking up. He'd be coming out of one of the central buildings and she'd see him staring. He'd turn away immediately, but she knew. He'd been watching her and she'd caught him. Just like the reverse happened sometimes.

Their only contact had been in the workouts he'd written down for her. She'd thought he'd forgotten about his promise to help her tone up. But nope, the morning after their breakup, she'd found a neatly written sheet of paper outlining simple toning exercises designed to be easy on her joints. They mostly involved water exercises, complete with special pads to add to the resistance when she swam. Those had appeared at her door that afternoon.

She wanted to thank him in person, but she never got close enough to him to actually speak. So she did the only thing she could. She worked out. Exactly as he instructed. And miracle of miracles, it was helping. Her body was stronger, the toning obvious. And her joints seemed to be handling the activity just fine.

Yeah. She'd be thrilled if only she could share her accomplishment with the man who'd made it all happen. But she couldn't, so she sabotaged herself with the cheesecake. Except even that couldn't hold a candle to the sight of Jason banging through laps in the pool.

"Excuse me. Are you Christy Baker?"

Christy looked up to see a crisp military uniform on a rather attractive woman with brown hair pulled into a severe bun. A lieutenant in the navy. And she was looking down at Christy with a hopeful expression.

"Um, yeah. I'm Christy."

"Do you mind if I join you for a minute?" She was already sitting down.

"Uh, sure."

"I'm Lt. Amelia Spark. I wondered if I might have a word with you about Capt. White."

Christy frowned, putting the pieces together fairly easily. "You're her. The navy shrink."

The woman smiled, though the expression was strained. "Yes. I'm a counselor here on base."

"You're *Jason's* counselor."

Lt. Spark gave an awkward shrug. "You understand that I can't confirm—"

"Or deny the relationship. Yeah, I get it." Christy sighed. She was too depressed to mince words. It wasn't rational for her to be jealous of the time Jason spent spilling his guts to this woman—this young, *attractive* woman—but she was. Irrationally jealous. And so she looked down at her cheesecake and gave it an angry stab.

Meanwhile, the woman shifted uncomfortably in her seat. "Okay, I'll be honest here. I'm walking a very fine line by talking to you at all, but I'm worried. So I'm bending the rules in the hopes that I can find some way to help."

Christy looked up, searching the woman's face for a sign of deception or dishonor or something. All she saw was honest concern. "You're worried about Jason."

Lt. Spark shifted uncomfortably again. Clearly she was a woman who fidgeted when nervous. "I can't confirm—"

"Right. But you are worried. And you came to ask me some questions. Fine." Her gaze drifted back to the pool and Jason's steady rhythm as each arm hit the water. "What do you want to know?"

"Are you still romantically involved with Capt. White?"

Christy shook her head. "No. He broke it off."

"Do you know why?"

She nodded again, but she didn't speak.

"Can you tell me?"

Christy frowned. "You don't know?"

Lt. Spark bit her lip, and Christy noted that one front tooth was slightly off center. She didn't know what it was about that tooth that suddenly made the woman seem more friendly. Perhaps because she was abruptly *not* crisp and perfect. Whatever the reason, Christy found herself relaxing a bit, especially in view of the woman's obvious anxiety.

"You understand that I can't talk about any of my clients."

"Of course, you can't. But you can ask, from one woman to another about my love life? All right. Yes, I know why Jason broke up with me. It's because he's a bullheaded, stubborn man. And because," she added with a heavy sigh, "he's probably right."

After all, they hadn't had any shared dreams since the breakup. Probably because they hadn't slept at the same time. And frankly, Christy hadn't slept well at all. Hard to believe she'd fallen so hard for a guy, so fast. They'd only really dated for two days. Two days, but damn, they were the best two days of her life.

Christy leaned back, and her thoughts walked the same tangle they'd wandered every day for the last week. "He told me before we started that he was messed up somehow. That he had amnesia, probably from getting blown up by an IED, and he hated it. He needed to remember something, and he couldn't."

She looked over to Lt. Spark, who had settled quietly into her seat now. This was probably how she looked when she was acting as a counselor: quiet, confident, a patient listener. Well, fine, maybe talking would help Christy sort things through.

"I told him he had to stop working so hard at it. Stop punishing himself." She gestured over to where Jason whipped around in the pool to start another lap. He'd probably stay in there for another hour before going on a grueling run along the beach. "He didn't listen. I was able to distract him for a while, I think. Good sex will do that for a guy, I guess." It had certainly distracted her.

"But it only lasted for a bit?"

Christy nodded. "He has good reasons, I suppose. But I also think his reasons are an excuse." How to explain this? She pushed away her half-eaten cheesecake to lean her arms forward on the table. She wanted to stare at something plain—like the white tablecloth—as she considered her thoughts.

"I'm a kindergarten teacher in my real life. Back in Ohio. There are these kids—great kids—but they're methodical. I see three main types of kids. Some are the social ones. I call them networkers—constantly moving, constantly talking. Others are hyper, highly distractable, hard to keep focused. Those I call my SAS kids, for short attention span. As in no ability to focus at all. Then there are the methodical ones. They do one thing at a time until they're done. Then they finish and go on to the next. Doesn't matter what my schedule is, they want to work at one thing, get it done, then move on. Linear steps. Amazing focus."

"Sounds like a good soldier."

She agreed. "It's not like they don't adapt. As they grow, they learn to split their focus, to manage different things at once, to accommodate my schedule and theirs. But at their core…"

"They like one thing at a time. Neat compartments, single focus."

Christy let her gaze shift to Jason. "I think that's how Jason is. It's not that we're not good together, or could have been." Honestly, they hadn't been together long enough to know if they were good for the long haul. "But his focus is on something else right now. And I just don't fit in."

"Sounds like it was as miracle you broke into his life at all."

Christy felt her lips twist into a wry smile. "I guess it was a kind of miracle." At least that was one way to describe shared erotic dreams.

Lt. Spark tapped her fingers on the table. She had blunt nails without polish, and bizarrely, Christy found she liked her more for it. She herself never had time for elaborate manicures. What would be the point? They'd just get chipped by blocks or dinosaur toys.

Meanwhile, the counselor started talking, carefully keeping her tone neutral. "The problem with methodical types, as you put it, is that they tend to get stuck. If they can't solve their problem—"

"They dig themselves in until they make everyone nuts. They start spinning their wheels, lose all sense of reality, and never get anywhere."

Ms. Sparks sighed. "It's the kind of focus that can move mountains, cure cancer or fly someone to the moon, but…"

"When they get stuck, they really entrench. It's hell on everyone until something breaks them out of it."

"It's especially hard on girlfriends. They sometimes don't have the understanding or experience to know how to handle it."

Christy sighed. "I have the experience. Just not the girlfriend status."

"Yeah. Guys can be such idiots sometimes."

They shared a smile of complete accord. But as the seconds ticked by, Christy put the pieces together. "You think that Jason has caught himself in a holding pattern and he needs something to break himself out."

"I would never suggest such a thing. But if I had a patient who I thought was spinning his wheels, I might suggest to that patient that he find some way to break the pattern. To do something different. Anything different."

Christy glanced at the pool. Sure enough, Jason was still churning away. "He's not listening."

"Marines, as a rule, are a stubborn bunch." Then once again, Lt. Sparks shifted uncomfortably on her seat. "Look, I'm not suggesting you do anything at all. I know next to nothing about you or your relationship with Capt. White. I just wanted some insight, is all. Answers as to why you two broke up."

"He's not talking to you at all, is he?" Christy asked. And then before the woman answered, she held up her hand. "I know, you can neither confirm nor deny." But somewhere deep inside, the petty part of her was relieved. This attractive woman had gotten no further with Jason than she had. But the non-petty part of her noted that Lt. Spark's worry was real. Which set off all kinds of worry inside Christy.

Meanwhile, Christy planted her chin on her palm and glared out the window. "Methodical types on a bad day can be…well, bad. They just lose it sometimes."

"I don't believe Capt. White is a danger to anyone," Lt. Spark stated firmly.

Christy was a little startled. "I wasn't thinking that at all. Jason would never hurt me. Hurt himself, however…"

The counselor straightened abruptly. "Do you think he's a danger to himself?"

"No, no! Not like you mean. I mean he's going to swim himself to exhaustion. Night after night of running, lifting, and I don't know what else he does. I thought exercise helped marines, but I've never seen him looking more grim. His eyes have that panicked look. And he's pushing his body to the very limits when he's supposed to be recuperating. If that's not the picture of a marine spinning his wheels, I don't know what is."

Which meant Jason needed someone to somehow get him out of his rut. Christy's mind was filling with things she could do, but then the therapist touched her hand.

"Please don't do anything rash. I just wanted to ask some questions. Get some answers, maybe. Not get you to do anything."

Christy didn't say a word, but her resolve had abruptly firmed. This holding pattern wasn't helping either of them. Jason was working himself to exhaustion, and Christy had spent the past couple weeks of her Hawaii summer being moody, depressed and love-sick. She needed to break the pattern even if he didn't.

She glanced up to Lt. Spark's worried face. "Don't worry, I'm not going to do anything," she lied. "I think I'll just sleep on it. Maybe take an afternoon nap."

12

JASON WAS PATROLLING that POS village again. His steps were the same, the sweat was the same, and so were the kids playing in what passed for a school yard. On some level he knew this was a dream. On another level entirely, he knew this was a memory that would soon end with him getting blown to hell. He knew it, fought it, but was powerless against the steady step of his feet.

The dream—and he—marched on. Until he took a step, shifted his weapon and found himself pointing it directly at Christy. She was wearing that yellow sundress again. His personal ray of sunshine in a very dark place. But she couldn't be here. It was dangerous!

"Damn it, Christy!" he cried as he tried to shield her with his body. But it was hard to do that when he didn't know where the enemy was. "Get behind me. Get down! It's dangerous here."

"No, it's not, Jason. It's a dream." She stepped around in front of him. "I want you to focus on me, Jason. Look at my face."

"What?"

"I used to play around with lucid dreaming in college. I've done more research lately, but here's the upshot. Focus on me. Remember that it's a dream."

He couldn't. He was still walking down that crappy road, the kids were still running and laughing to their right, and any minute now he was going to get into his jeep and get blown to hell. He couldn't look at Christy. He was looking for something else.

But she wouldn't let him be. The damn woman stepped right in front of him again, took his face between her hands and kissed him.

He fought her. This wasn't the time, but she stepped into his arms and whispered, "Just go with it," just before she attached herself to his mouth.

Part of him fought. It was the part that was still step by step walking to the jeep. But no way had he ever been able to break one of Christy's kisses. It was like kissing freedom, and the greater part of him surrendered to her.

The kiss deepened and his gun fell to the side. He wrapped his arm around her, hauling her up against him. She giggled. He felt the joy of it rumble through his body and he found himself smiling as he never thought he would in this hellhole.

Then she pulled back and spoke, her words making no sense at all. "It's too hot here. Let's go back to the beach."

He frowned. "Can't. We're looking for—"

"Don't tell me what you're doing. I don't want to know. And besides, we absolutely can." Then she took a deep breath and waved her arms. She moved fluidly, without any of the stiffness he'd seen at other times. She waved her arms, then spun in a happy circle. And around her the scenery changed to a moonlit Hawaiian beach.

"There!" she said as she came to a stop. "See! It's called lucid dreaming, and we can create it however we want."

He looked around, but it was wrong. All wrong. She shouldn't be here. And he had something important to do. He closed his eyes, trying to sort through his sluggish thoughts, and when he opened them again, he was back in that crap village complete with run-down shacks and kids that seemed like they would play chase and tag games until the world ended. He was looking for a bioweapons factory. They had to find it now. It was important, damn it, and he couldn't be pulled off the mission to play on a Hawaiian beach.

"There's something I have to do," he said firmly.

She sighed. "Yes, I know. But not right now. You've been dreaming this for two weeks straight. Longer, probably. Today, you get a break."

He shook his head. Why wouldn't she listen? "I have to—"

"Focus on me, Jason. You have to focus on me. I don't belong in this village, do I?"

"Definitely not!"

"Then put me where I do belong."

He didn't understand, and then the jeep was coming. He could hear the motor as it came to pick him up. Any minute now he would climb in—

"Jason! Where do I belong? Look at me and think of where I belong. We'll go there together."

He looked at her then. He could hardly resist her with that bright yellow sundress. She was right. She didn't belong here. She was meant to be in a house with kids running around. She'd be baking cookies while the baby slept. And on the kitchen table would be papers she was grading or the next day's school lessons. In short, she belonged in a *home*, not in this pit.

And just like that, the scenery changed. He saw a beautiful kitchen with flowers on the table and peanut butter and jelly sandwiches on the counter. A pair of kids ran through—a boy and a girl—and he jumped backward, pulling his gun out of the way. He was still dressed in his fatigues, and he sure as hell didn't belong here.

But Christy did. That sundress fit perfectly with the light streaming in through the window over the sink. She was looking around, pulling off two big lobster-claw oven mitts as she stared at him in horror.

"Holy moly, I've landed in a sixties sitcom." She looked at him. "Is this seriously how you picture me?"

He nodded, his belly tight with longing. This was the home he'd always wanted as a kid. And she was the wife he'd always pictured. Sweet, nurturing, and so damn sexy in that yellow sundress.

She looked at his face, and her expression softened. "Classic TV mom fantasy it is." But when she went close to him, he stepped back.

"I should go. I don't belong here."

"Yes, you do. It's *your* dream."

He looked around at the white countertops, smelled the sweet scent of chocolate-chip cookies, and almost gave in. But then a dirty kid ran through the room. He was Filipino and he stumbled, scraping his knee on the linoleum floor even though there was nothing there to trip him up. Then he straightened with a grin.

Jason had to follow that kid, and so he grabbed his

weapon and moved after him. The room started to shift again. Already he could feel the heat and grime, something that would never be in that kitchen. Then Christy grabbed his arm, drawing him back to face her.

"Don't go, Jason. Don't shut me out. Or yourself out. Or whatever." She stretched up to press her lips to his. "Come on. You put me in this sundress, don't leave me here with the kids when you so obviously want to be here, too."

"What?"

She smiled. "I can feel your longing. It's in every breath of this dream. You want to be here with me."

Suddenly, the kitchen door opened and there he was, walking in, wearing a suit and a thin tie. "Honey, I'm home!"

Christy spun around and frowned at him. Except it wasn't him. It was a robot him with plastic skin and a vacant expression.

"You are *not* leaving me here with him," Christy snapped.

"I don't belong here," Jason said. "And I have something important to do."

"You are *not* leaving me here!" She spun around, squarely turning her back on his double. "Jason, this is a *dream*. You control it. What do you want to see?"

"I don't belong—"

"Yes, you do! You belong wherever you want to be." She stepped up close, filling his entire vision with her face, her warm eyes, her full wet lips. "What do you want, Jason?"

He didn't speak. He didn't open his mouth, but even he could hear the word echo through the room. "You."

She smiled and opened her arms wide. "Then

take me. I'm right here for you." She reached up to his shoulder and gently lifted off his backpack. "You should put this down. It's probably heavy."

He didn't shift to help her. If anything, he tightened his shoulders, but she was relentless. And soon, he felt so much better without his pack.

"And you don't need that anymore," she said, pointing at his weapon.

He thumbed on the safety and set it aside, a little ashamed that he had it out here.

"You need to relax a little before you explode. Want a glass of wine? Dinner? I think there are peanut butter and jelly sandwiches over there."

He didn't even look at the counter. All he wanted was her. But something was holding him back. Some part of him still fought this dream.

"I haven't finished the other thing yet," he said.

"I know. But you'll get to it tomorrow."

He shook his head. "One thing at a time. One—"

"Do you want to make love here? Or do you want to wake up and do it for real?"

He blinked, his mind struggling for focus. Especially as she pulled herself up on the counter, her legs dangling free, her skirt suddenly a lot shorter than he remembered. God, she had great legs.

She smiled at him and his mind went fuzzy. She was so beautiful. He wanted her with an ache that filled his entire soul. But just as he took a step for her, he heard the sound. The jeep engine.

He felt himself climb in, his shirt sticking to his back. It was hot as hell here.

"No, Jason!"

And then he was driving down the road. He knew

what was coming, and try as he might, he couldn't stop it.

"Wait! I know where it is!" he said to Danny.

Christy screamed something. She even grabbed his arm, but it was too late. They hit the IED and the world went white with pain.

CHRISTY WOKE with a gasp, her head throbbing and an ache in her gut that was starting to fade. It was Jason's wound site, she was sure. Where shrapnel had torn into his body. She was feeling the echo of his nightmare, and hell, it hurt.

She pushed up from her bed, rapidly orienting herself. She'd gone to her room, expressly intent on slipping into Jason's dreams. She'd meant to help him get unstuck. She hadn't had any clear idea how, except that a change—any change—might do the trick.

With that thought in mind, she'd settled in for a nap. And then, miracle of miracles, it had worked. She'd slipped into his nightmare and talked him into changing it. Thank God for her college experimentation with lucid dreaming. She doubted she could have done that without the practice back then.

Either way, it had worked. Right up until the point where he'd blown them sky-high in that jeep. And now he was probably waking up the same way she was, only on the opposite side of the wall. He would be drenched in sweat, shaking, and struggling to remember what they'd dreamed.

If she was lucky, he'd remember very little. If she wasn't...

She heard the banging first. He was storming through the kitchenette. She'd left her door unlocked, so she had no time to prepare. One second she heard him come through the kitchen, then next second her door was slammed against the wall and he stood there in nothing but loose boxer shorts. His hair was messed, his face was haggard, and his eyes were wild.

"Was that you?" he gasped. "Was that on purpose?"

She never even considered lying. "Yes. On both counts."

"God damn it, Christy!" He stomped across the room. He grabbed her by the arms. "How dare you do that to me!"

There were a thousand answers to that question. A thousand half-truths or outright lies that could have tumbled from her lips. But he was right there in front of her. And he was losing it by the second. So she said the first thing that came to mind. Sadly, it was also the bald truth.

"I had to. I think I'm falling in love with you."

13

Jason felt her words hit him like a ton of bricks. She thought she was falling in love with him? Jesus. This was too much. He already felt like he was sitting on a land mine, his every cell ratcheted up to the point that he was going to explode. And he did. Nightly in that damn jeep. And then into his nightmare walks this ray of sunshine, who says she's falling in love? It was too much. IED, amnesia, shared dreams and then this? He couldn't handle it.

His hands started shaking, and then his belly cramped. She was looking at him with her heart in her eyes, and all he could do was stand there fighting the pain.

"Jason? Say something."

"Turn around." His throat was clenched tight, but he forced the words out.

"What?"

"Turn around!"

She flinched at his tone, and he silently cursed himself. "Please," he said, trying to be gentle. "I don't want— You can't see— Not when I'm like this.

Please." He closed his eyes and pressed his fists to his eyes. "Don't look at me."

She touched his fist, her fingers so tender it made his knees weak. "You think I haven't seen a man in pain before? Jason, you've been heading for this for weeks now. I had to—"

He threw off her fingers, grabbed her by the waist and spun her around. She gasped in surprise, but he didn't hurt her. He made damn sure he didn't hurt her. He just wanted to hold her, but away from him. She couldn't be looking at him right now. He didn't want to see her doe eyes or her sweet halo of brown hair.

I think I'm falling in love with you.

It was too much to process. Not when he had other things on his plate. Not when people's lives hung in the balance. His damn memory. A bioweapons factory making something that could kill half a city in a blink of an eye. And yet the more he thought of that, the more he remembered her words.

I think I'm falling in love with you.

She couldn't. He couldn't. And yet she was here in his arms.

"Jason, it's okay. It's going to be okay."

He nodded, tucking his chin against her neck, her bottom against his groin. She was soft and she felt so damn good. He closed his eyes and breathed deep. She smelled like some fruity shampoo and herself. She was wearing shorts and a loose tee. He slipped his fingers underneath her shirt to stroke her smooth belly. She touched the back of his hands through her shirt. It was only a light press, but he felt it like he felt that IED explode beneath the jeep. Everything went white and his whole body screamed.

Except this was a good scream, though just as painful. His breath rasped and he tightened his grip. His entire body was tight with the need to thrust into her, but he couldn't move. He was too afraid—it would mean so much. He just needed to hold her. Just. Hold. Her.

"Something's going to break, Jason. Something in *you* if you don't let go."

He took a breath. It hurt to inhale with her scent right there, her body right here. But he did it, and when he exhaled the pain might have been less. It was hard to tell. But she was right here, and he was touching her.

"I don't know what's going on in your head, Jason, but I want to help. Tell me what you need."

"You," he said. "Just you."

"Okay."

His hands skimmed up her rib cage. He pulled back enough to reach the clasp of her bra and pop it open. Then he pulled both shirt and bra off her body with one quick move. She was trapped, her legs caught against the bed, him pressing against her from behind, pinning her in place while he touched every part of her upper body.

Belly, waist, breasts. God, he loved holding her breasts. She shuddered in his arms as he played with her nipples. He thumbed them, took them between his fingers and tugged. And all the while, he listened to her sounds. Gasps, soft cries, even a keening moan.

"Jason—" she began.

"Don't talk," he whispered. "I know I'm an ass—"

"No—"

"And I swear I'll talk. I swear. I just—" He pressed his lips to her shoulder, smelling her sweet scent, seeing her creamy white skin, and most of all filling his senses with her. "Just let me do this right now."

"Methodical Jason. One thing at a time." He felt her smile. He felt her whole body soften. Or maybe he just felt her and how damn beautiful she was.

He pressed another kiss to her shoulder, this time closer to her neck. And while he was there, he tasted her, filling himself with her.

He pushed her forward a bit. And she responded in kind.

He tongued her spine and let his teeth scrape gently across the bumps from her vertebrae. He shaped her breasts, and then he moved lower still. Her belly trembled, but he didn't stop there. He was kissing between her shoulder blades and unfastening her shorts at the same time. A second later, he was able to push them down so that she was completely naked.

He nudged her forward even more. The slightest resistance and he would have stopped. But she took his cues without hesitation. She bent at the waist and braced her hands on the bed. Gently he urged her to step wider.

She did. And while he was pressing kisses down her spine, he slipped a finger between her legs.

Sweet heaven, she was wet. She was hot and moist and he'd never felt anything so sweet as the moisture between her slick folds.

She arched, stretching her back and releasing a low moan. He used his left hand to fondle a breast, her beautiful full breast. His right hand stayed in her wet heat. He penetrated then pulled out, stroking every part of her, while she gasped and writhed beneath him.

He wanted to be inside her. His dick was like granite. But he wouldn't do anything to change what was happening right then. She was building to her climax. He felt her legs quiver, knew it when her shoulder blades tensed and her spine did a slow roll. He felt her every stuttering breath as he stroked her.

His Christy.

"Jason!" she gasped. God, he loved it when she called his name. He craved it like a drug.

"Jason! Come with me!" She turned her head, tried to reach for the bedside table and the condoms in the drawer. But he didn't let her move and couldn't find the words to explain.

This wasn't about him. This wasn't even about sex. This was about him holding her, about giving her the only thing he could. Pleasure. Ecstasy.

So he stroked her more. And held her beneath him, touching her the best way he could. He drew out the building tension. She cried out, panting. He stroked her high again then held off just before the release.

She was shaking beneath him, her body like a wild thing in his arms. And then when he knew she couldn't take it anymore, he finished her. He pinched her clit, and she screamed. It wasn't his name this time. Just a single scream. But he held it in his heart, just as he held her in his heart.

Falling in love? Hell, he was in so deep, he'd never see daylight again.

CHRISTY GROANED, but it was a happy groan. She'd collapsed onto her bed, her body completely limp after an orgasm the likes of which she'd never even imagined before, let alone experienced. He'd been a master, caging her between his arms, touching her everywhere at once.

And now she lay boneless on the bed while he remained rigidly poised above her. She could hear his breath, amazingly steady, at least compared to the hammering of her heart. There were a lot of things she wanted to say to him. A lot of things *he* needed to say, period. Never had she met a man who wound himself so tight.

But at the moment, only one thing was on her mind. One sentence, but she made sure he heard every word. "If you do not put on a condom this second, I will never, ever forgive you."

She felt her words hit him. She felt his surprise at her words, and then, finally, he opened her bedside drawer.

She didn't move as he ripped open the packet. She'd barely managed to gather the strength to shift on the bed. Thankfully, he was strong. He held her hips and settled her into position.

And then he was home. Pushed in in one long slide. She loved this feeling. He stretched her, he filled her, and it was a joy to open up to him. Plus, she knew he liked it when she said his name, so she made a point of saying it.

"You're perfect, Jason. This is so perfect."

He didn't answer. She didn't expect him to. She had a guess as to why. Strong silent types kept it all inside. But he'd promised he'd talk. She could tell she'd broken his tailspin. Or at least she thought she had.

And in the meantime, he was thrusting inside her. A long, steady push, then a slow, aching withdrawal. In and out. Methodical. And amazing.

His hands found her breasts again. He was going to do it again to her. He wasn't the kind of man to take his pleasure without a thought for hers. She opened her mouth to tell him not to worry about her. She'd just had the best orgasm of her life. She certainly didn't need to do it again so soon. But he was relentless. And he knew just how to touch her.

He tugged on her nipple. Just one, but he had those magic fingers.

"Jason—" she gasped. It was a last-ditch attempt to keep some sanity. This was supposed to be for him. But she should have known better. She'd said his name, and his intensity increased.

His thrusts went from slow and deep, to faster and hotter. She arched her back, willing him to take what he wanted.

But he was determined. And before she could say another thing, his hand left her breast to slip between her folds. He didn't have to do more than slide his finger between her cleft. His thrusts did the rest.

Hard. And harder still. Forward and backward. Sheer heaven.

Her body tightened.

His tempo increased.

One more!

One—

"Jason!"

Yes!

14

"I NEVER REALIZED afternoon naps could be so much fun." Christy smiled as she said it, then pressed a kiss to Jason's glorious chest. They were lying on her bed, nearly in the position they'd collapsed in after that last unforgettable orgasm.

He had recovered first. She'd been happy to have him pressing down on top of her for, oh, an aeon or so. But he'd groaned and rolled to the side. Then he'd slipped an arm under her legs and lifted her up onto the bed. She hadn't the energy to do more than murmur her thanks.

Then he got into bed beside her, spooned her tight against him, and then…then they'd both fallen asleep. For three hours. A sweet dreamless sleep that they both had needed.

But now she was awake, and so she'd turned around. She wanted to see his face. Wanted to press kisses into his chest. And she wanted him to keep his promise. Not for her sake. For his.

"Jason," she said as she pushed up onto one arm. "You promised you'd talk."

He was looking at her, his blue eyes dark in the late-afternoon sun. There was some light in the room, but it shadowed his gaze. She touched his face, stroking a thumb beneath his eyes, feeling the chiseled angle of his jaw and cheekbone.

She smiled, trying for a light tone. "Time to man up, marine."

"I know."

She waited a moment. He was clearly working his way to the words, but it remained hard for him. She knew she had to break the tension somehow, so she lifted off his body to look him squarely in the eye.

"Do you know who the scariest person on the planet is?"

His eyebrows went up. "Who?"

"Not you badass marines, though God knows you try." She saw his lips twitch in the beginnings of a smile. Progress! "No, the scariest thing on the planet is a kindergarten teacher."

"Really?"

"Really. Think back. Ever do something bad in the sandbox? Stole somebody's truck or punched a girl."

"I'd never hit a girl."

"Even if she hit you first?"

He grimaced. "Okay. Maybe if she hit me first. And could take a punch."

She nodded. "Damn straight you would." There were women in the military, and they'd be pissed as hell at any macho attitude like that. "So, macho man, what evil thing did you do in kindergarten?"

He had to think hard, but he found it. "I punched Joey Whitaker in the nose."

She reared back in pretend shock. "You hoodlum. What'd he do?"

"Punched a girl."

She smiled. "Of course he did." So Jason was a protector even at the ripe age of five. "What'd your teacher do?"

He shuddered. It was a real shudder, too, his eyes widened in surprise. "She came down on me like the wrath of God."

"See what I mean? Scariest thing. Kindergarten teachers."

"No argument here."

She straightened and gave him her best teacher glare. "So, young man, I believe you made me a promise earlier."

He nodded gravely. "Yes, ma'am, I did."

"I expect you to honor that promise."

He swallowed, but he held her gaze. Finally, he forced the words out. They came in a slow methodical march while his body tightened with tension against her. He didn't blink as he spoke.

"I can't remember, Christy. People's lives depend on me remembering. Maybe a whole lot of lives, but I can't do it."

She released her breath slowly. This much she already knew, but there was more. She was sure of it. "Keep going," she urged.

He rubbed his palm over his face. "There isn't anything more. There's just—"

"Bull hockey. There's me. Why are you fighting me so hard?"

He swallowed, his expression shifting to panicked.

But to his credit, his never looked away. "You're a distraction—"

"Good try, but wrong. You're the most focused man I know. You can block me out without even blinking."

He snorted. "You underestimate your charms."

"And you think I'm not a scary kindergarten teacher. But I can guarantee you that I am. So look deeper, marine, or no more recess for you. For a whole month."

"A whole month, huh? That is scary."

"Damn straight." She sobered. They had reached a lighter tone, but this was too important for him to give up now. "Why do you keep running from me?"

"I'm in your bed, Christy—"

"Because I had to drag you here." She grimaced. "Metaphorically speaking."

"And yeah, we're still going to have to talk about how you hopped into my dream again."

Okay, score one for him. That was one discussion she really didn't want to have. "Fine. But we're having this one first. What's so terrible about me that you're fighting it so hard?"

"Because you're perfect. Because you're a kindergarten teacher and gorgeous. Because you represent mom and apple pie and all the things I've been fighting to protect for all these years."

"And that's scary?"

"I've been fighting for other people, Christy. I'm the warrior. They're the happy ones."

She stilled, slowly fitting his words with what she already knew about him. He was methodical, doing one thing, finishing it, then moving on. That personality also tended to see things as black and white. Good or bad. Happy or not.

"So, warriors fight, civilians enjoy."

He tilted his head in silent agreement.

"And warriors can't be happy?"

He sighed. "Not the way civilians are."

She had grown up on one military base after another. She did understand the military mind-set. At least in part. His attitude wasn't unique, but it certainly wasn't the only perspective.

"Military people get married all the time. They live happy lives with wives and children, and still find a way to serve their country."

"Ever seen a wife find out that her husband is dead? Ever seen the kids get the news?"

She nodded. "A couple times." Given her childhood, that was probably two more times than he had. After all, he was the one on deployment. She'd been one of the kids left behind to wait and worry. "But millions of people do it every day. A loved one goes to a dangerous job. The rest of the family prays that they'll come back. What makes you so special?"

He shook his head. "Not special. Realistic."

It was a lie. She could tell it by the way his body flinched even as he said the words. They were still pressed tightly together. She felt the way he breathed. No way could he tell her a lie like that and not get exposed.

"Try again, Jason. Tell me what you really believe."

Now he did try to look away, but she was faster than he was. She had her palm to his chin and she held him in place. He could have thrown her off, of course, but he didn't. In the end, his words rasped out with an angry huff.

"It's just not for me, okay? Mom and apple pie, it's never been for me."

She mulled over his words and intonation. It wasn't like "it's never been for me" because he wasn't into it, like he might not care for reggae or lemon meringue pie. It was more like, I don't deserve it or I don't get to have that.

It took her a while to get to that understanding. What came first from him was pain. Anguish, maybe. The kind that settled into a boy at a really young age. And then it festered, steadily eating into his soul.

"When did you start thinking that you couldn't be happy? That you weren't a person who could ever be happy?"

He opened his mouth, probably to deny it, but she held his gaze.

"Think, Jason. Someone, sometime told you you couldn't ever be happy. Who was it?"

"My father," he murmured, and she could tell he was remembering it even as he told her the story. "He was a truck driver and a mean drunk. There was one night. He was on his second six-pack and I was… I don't know. Six? Seven?"

"What did he do?"

He shook his head. "Not do. Said. He said folks like us weren't cut out for good times. Happy was for other people."

"Mom and apple pie."

He nodded. "He said we just suffered. We did the work while others built their lives on our backs."

She grimaced. Jason's father wasn't the first parent she wanted put in mandatory therapy, and he certainly wouldn't be the last.

Meanwhile, Jason continued. "Dad was an ass and a drunk. He was always spouting shit."

"And you know how words can settle into a kid, right? Even if they know it's crap on a conscious level, it still sinks deep. Some part of them believes it always. Unless…"

He turned to her, and she thought she saw hope spark in his eyes. Or maybe she just wanted to see it. Maybe she wanted to believe she could reach him.

"Unless?" he asked.

"Unless you make a conscious decision to believe something else. Something like you *do* deserve to be happy. That you *can* be a warrior and happy. It *is* possible for you."

He stared at her, and she could see him wishing her words were true. Just as she prayed he could believe it.

"Believe in me, Jason. If nothing else, believe what I'm telling you now and telling that little six-year-old boy who was listening too closely to his drunken father. You deserve happiness. And more than that, you can have it. Mom, apple pie, even the sixties television sitcom—though I'd suggest you try to update that a bit. It's all possible for you. You just have to believe you can."

She saw the yearning in his eyes, felt it in the tension in his body. Beliefs held this deeply didn't change overnight, but they did shift. They did start to change between one breath and the next. Was this that moment for him?

"Christy."

"Yes?"

He shook his head. "Nothing. Just…Christy." Then he kissed her. Deep, powerful and passionate.

She responded in kind, needing to hold him, wanting to impress everything she believed into his body. They barely got the condom on him before he was inside her again. Hard. Hot.

"Jason!"

Yes!

15

A MONTH LATER, she was still breathless, though for an entirely different reason. They were doing her morning exercises in the pool, and she was struggling. So she grabbed for a conversation topic to distract her.

"So I'm supposed to chaperone the sock hop. And poor me, I have no date." Christy said the words without inflection, partly because she had no breath to put intonation into her words. She was walking laps in the water. Yes, walking. Jason was holding her hand and doing the same beside her, looking all sleek and relaxed, but she was gasping and straining because, damn, walking in a swimming pool was *hard*. It was also very easy on her joints, and that was very good.

"No date?" he echoed, though with plenty of inflection because he wasn't even huffing. "To a sock hop? Didn't those go out in the fifties?"

"Along with afternoon sundaes, but the MWR is putting one on. Haven't you seen the fliers? Sundaes on the beach, luau with flame dancers, and then—"

"A sock hop? On the beach?"

"I am *not* on the planning committee. Do I look

like a Morale, Welfare and Recreation lackey?" She abruptly held up her hand. "Don't answer that! I'm just a chaperone without a date." She heaved a heavy sigh that was half drama, half a way to catch her breath as they turned around and headed back the other way. She'd hoped he would stop them at the end of this lap, but he just kept smiling at her as they kept going.

"I'd kill to see you in a grass skirt."

"Not appropriate chaperone attire."

"Huh." His face took on a dreamy expression, and she splashed him to get his attention.

"What were you thinking?"

He flashed her a grin. "Just about chaperone-appropriate attire. And how I would love to get you out of it."

"Hush!" She glanced around. It was early yet, before the families came out to swim. Her class wasn't until ten, so they'd shifted her morning workout to the pool. But that didn't mean she wanted to publicize some of the very scandalous things they'd been doing together over the past month. For all that having a hot navy fling had been on her agenda for this summer, it didn't mean she wanted to advertise it to her clients' parents. "Come on, Jason. Will you be my date on Sunday?"

He took a moment, obviously thinking ahead to whether he could risk making plans three days in the future. She'd already learned that he wouldn't commit to anything a week away, but she thought she'd be okay with a commitment seventy-two hours in advance.

"Well," he drawled, obviously toying with her. "I'd love to be your date on Sunday, but that's not what I'd be doing. I'd be watching out for kids spiking the punch, or interrupting beer guzzling and teenage snog fests."

She almost choked on her laughter. "Snog fest?"

"Yeah, you know. Snogging. Kissing." He put on a mock insulted look. "It's a Britishism."

"But you wouldn't—"

"I would. That's what chaperones—and their dates—do."

She thought about it. It was true. As a kindergarten teacher she never had to worry about teenage antics. She worried about kids putting frogs in the punch, not cheap whiskey. Huh. She would have to change her whole mind-set. Meanwhile, he kept on talking.

"I don't know. It'll feel kinda hypocritical to be preventing teenage snogging when I'm thinking about doing the same thing with the teacher."

"The teacher is an adult. The kids—"

"Usually try to get their beer from me."

She stumble-stepped, but he easily kept her upright. Then she thought about what he said and called him on it. "That can't be true. You're not usually stationed here."

He dipped his head in agreement. "True, but wherever I am, every teen seems to think I'd be willing to help them skirt the rules."

"You're not, are you? Or you won't. At least, while we're together."

"I don't. I won't. I swear."

"Good, 'cause I'm supposed to be an example of moral rectitude." Then before he could react, she leveled a finger at his nose. "Do not laugh at that. There are some requirements of teachers. Especially ones who intend to apply for this job again next summer."

He nodded gravely. "I understand, ma'am. No beer. No moral corruption. I will be the model of propriety." He said it with a straight face, all while backing her up against the pool wall. Because of the early hour, they were relatively alone, even in an outdoor pool, so she decided to let him kiss her. In truth, she was nearly breathless with the desire he stoked in her. Wet, rippling chest, rosy morning sunlight in his eyes, and his mouth bare inches from hers.

She lifted her mouth for his kiss. God, she couldn't get enough of this man. He drew out the temptation, hovering just a scant breath away. And then...

He scooped her up and threw her halfway across the pool. Damn, he was strong! She landed with a yelp and a splash. As she spit out a mouthful of water, he shrugged.

"A morally correct gentleman does not kiss a lady. Certainly not in public."

"Is that your way of accepting my date request?" she sputtered as she wiped the water from her eyes.

"It's my way of getting you to start swimming. Walk time is over. Now it's swim time."

She frowned. "But I've done my half hour—"

"You've got extra time this morning. I checked your schedule."

"Do not!" she lied.

"Do to! I'm a marine and we're very thorough. So I know the truth. Now get swimming! Because if I catch you, then there will be consequences."

She grinned. She liked the sound of that.

"And they will be morally upstanding consequences."

Oh, hell. That didn't sound fun at all.

She waited long enough to see that he was serious. Then with a muttered curse, she flung her body into slow, awkward strokes. Swimming might be easier on her joints than running, but that didn't mean it was *easy*.

Still, with him chasing her, she didn't seem to mind. Exercise had never been so much fun.

SUNDAES ON THE BEACH weren't so bad, Jason thought as he took a heaping spoonful of his ice cream. Chocolate ice cream with chocolate fudge and chocolate sprinkles, along with a chocolate chip cookie. He was a man of simple tastes.

Christy raised her eyebrows at his sugar intake and sighed as she nibbled on a carrot stick. He laughed and picked up another huge scoop.

"As your personal trainer, I can tell you with absolute assurance that your body needs this now." He waved the dripping ice cream in front of her.

She rolled her eyes. "I'll go into sugar shock. And gain seven pounds."

"I promise to make you work it off later."

She eyed him, her lips pursing in a delightful pout. "In a morally upstanding workout?"

"Definitely not."

"Oh, well, in that case." She leaned forward and seductively wrapped her tongue around the spoon before pulling it into her mouth. Wow. Just the sight of that had him thinking of throwing her over his shoulder and taking her back to his cave.

"Keep that up," he warned, "and you won't make it long enough to chaperone the dance."

"Hmm, you do know how to tempt a girl." And

then just to prove that she could push his restraint to the very edge, she got up and walked away...with a very distinct swivel to her hips. The fact that she was wearing a bright-yellow-and-blue swimsuit and a long sarong made his lust surge like high tide. Especially since she was moving more easily than at the beginning of the summer. Her new muscle tone was obvious, her joints were paining her less, and...well, she just looked good to him. All bright summer happiness bottled into one sexy package.

He didn't know where she was going or why she was walking away. But a second later, he saw that she was joining the same pack of preteens he'd met at the beginning of the summer. And just like six weeks ago, Judy was hovering on the edge looking just as unsure as before.

Christy said something to the girl, and the child brightened immediately. But the second Christy's attention was diverted elsewhere, the girl slid back into hanger-on status. God, it was hard to watch. He just ached for the girl. Funny how he probably would have never noticed it before, but suddenly he had paternal instincts for a girl he'd never even met. A month with Christy had changed his perspective on a lot of things, including preteen angst.

Fortunately, he'd done some research. Nothing obvious, and he'd stumbled on the information more out of luck than anything else. But a few days ago he'd learned a little about science fiction-fantasy fandom, and who was knee-deep in it. Now that he had the knowledge, it was time to act. He pushed to his feet, snagging a water bottle on the way so he had an excuse to join them.

"Got this for you," he said to Christy as he handed her the bottle of water. She smiled her thanks, but there was a question in her eyes. He just winked back at her and turned to Judy. "Hey, you're Judy Walker, aren't you?"

The girl nodded.

"I heard that your uncle worked on the set of *Firefly*. That you even got to hang out with Joss Whedon for a day. And imagine, I know someone who spent two grand just so he could sit in the audience, and you got to hang out with the guy."

Now the truth was, he didn't know *Firefly* from *Babylon 5,* which made him a major loser in some crowds. Specifically Ryan Taylor's crowd. He was the clear leader of the group of teenagers who were standing right next to Judy. Apparently the kid had a comic book collection almost as large as his sci-fi book collection. And that was nothing compared to his DVDs and whatever, all written by the creator of *Buffy the Vampire Slayer.*

Meanwhile, Judy's eyes widened at Jason's attention, but she stumbled into a nod. "Y-yeah. Joss was nice. We talked about his stuff. But mostly he asked me about school and my ideas. He was, you know, a real guy."

"You know Joss Whedon?" Ryan gasped. "Like for real?"

Judy turned, obviously startled that the coolest guy there was looking at her with awe. Jason grinned. It took only a few more minutes before the two were talking Whedon comics versus Whedon television. Which spun into other sci-fi something or other and Comicons and… Hell, he didn't know the lingo. But obviously those two did. And right before their eyes, a friendship was born.

Feeling very pleased with himself, he glanced at Christy. "Hey, you wanna get some barbeque?"

His girl blinked at him, her attention still riveted on the changes in Judy. He had to admit, even he was surprised at how quickly Judy blossomed out of her nervous, shy persona now that she had something to talk about with someone who was interested.

"Um, sure," Christy mumbled.

He took her hand and started leading her away. She watched the group as long as she could without being obvious, and then he had her all to himself again. Which was exactly what he wanted.

"How'd you know?" she asked him.

"What?"

"About the *Firefly* thing?"

"Hmm? Oh, chatted with her dad a couple weeks ago. And Ryan's obviously the leader of that little group. So I asked *his* dad just…um…last Monday… what the kid's passion was."

"Looking for a common interest between the two?"

He nodded. "I had no idea just how space-geek the two were, but it looks like it fits." He glanced back to where the two had wandered off together. They were both talking animatedly, complete with hand gestures that might have been suggestive but was probably Wookiee speak or something.

"You're amazing."

"Yeah, it's nice when things click."

She laughed, and his attention turned back to her. "No, stupid. I said *you're* amazing. Not them. You."

She was looking at him with awe. As if he held the

moon and the stars in his hand, and he just stared at her in shock. This was the woman who held his hand when he woke up sweating from his nightmares. This was the woman who had dragged him out of his self-imposed isolation and opened her body and her heart to him. This was the woman who called him stupid with one breath and yet could look at him like that.

His breath caught. What had he ever done to deserve that look? The idea sparked panic in his chest on a completely irrational level. What if he failed her?

He swallowed. "Don't do that," he said as he started walking along the beach. He still held her hand, so she stayed by his side, but he could tell he had confused her.

"Do what?" she asked.

"Well…" He glanced at her again and winced. The sun was sparking the honey streaks in her hair to gold, and she was laughing at him. But the worship was still there. "Act like that. Like I'm a hero or something."

She bumped his shoulder with hers. "Well, maybe you are a hero."

"I just found out something stupid about a kid. It was nothing."

"It was more than nothing to Judy. And frankly, it was a lot more than most people would do. I've been working all summer to find a way to help her, and you did it without a second thought."

"Right place at the right time," he muttered. "That's all."

"I hear you marines make a habit of being at the right place at the right time."

He sighed and turned to face her, his expression sober. "Christy, just don't do that. Don't put me on a pedestal. Not because I'm a marine, not because I said something nice to some kid. Just...don't."

She stopped, digging her heels into the sand as her smile faded to something a breath short of annoyance. "I wouldn't do that. Put you on some pedestal. Or the corps. What's going on, Jason? Why are you suddenly all prickly?"

He rubbed a hand over his face. Was it him? Or was this something that had been building between them for a while now? "You do that a lot. Look at me like I'm some sort of amazing gift. Not right now," he grumbled. "But before. And other times. You look at me like—"

"Like a woman in love?"

"No!" He didn't know if he was objecting to the idea of her loving him or that was her look. Good God, how had this afternoon spun out of control so fast?

"Jason, take a breath. What's—"

He gripped her arms, looking at her closely as he struggled for the right words. "Forget me, Christy. What is it in you that looks at a man like that? It's not love, Christy. Or not completely. It's—"

"It's an I-can't-believe-a-guy-like-you-is-with-a-girl-like-me look." She said the words almost deadpan. And worse, her gaze was sliding away as if she couldn't face him.

"Yeah," he said. "Like that."

She started walking, and now he was the one keeping pace with her. "I get what you're saying. And for the record, there was no pedestal."

"No, it's that other thing you just said. Why couldn't you get a guy like me? Really, I'm not that—"

"Hot? Drop-dead gorgeous? A hero in the military

sense and also caring enough to be my trainer even when we were arguing? Oh, plus, you helped out a kid you don't even know."

He groaned. Didn't she understand those things were nothing? They were easy.

She groaned right back at him, exaggerating the sound. "Look, I know you've got problems. You're still waking up every other night on the edge of a scream. And God knows if I ever bring up any plans beyond a couple days, you run for the hills."

"I do not—"

"You do, too. So no, no pedestal. You're only a Greek god in bed."

He flashed her a grin. He was okay with that kind of hero worship. But the expression quickly faded. "So why the…" What had she said? "I-can't-believe-a-guy-like-you—"

"Yeah." She cut him off. "I know what I said."

He waited with an eyebrow raised. He recognized evasion when he saw it. After all, he was a master of it himself. But with her, all he had to do was wait it out. Eventually she'd tell him. And sure enough, she shrugged and started walking again, her words timed with her steps.

"Summer fling, remember? Nothing permanent. You said that, too. So I got exactly what I hoped for—a summer romance with a guy too hot to believe."

His gut clenched at the thought of this being over by the end of the summer. But the truth was, this was over the second he remembered what he needed to. His body was almost fully recovered. It was only his mind that everyone was waiting on.

"So what's the problem?" he asked, even though he

knew exactly what the issue was. It could end at any second. But then she said something completely unexpected.

"Who gets a summer fling like this? I mean, we all talk about having the hottie for the summer. Sex with wild abandon. Naked on the beach time."

"For the record, we haven't done that. Yet."

She shot him a glance. "We did in our dreams."

Oh, yeah. He'd forgotten about that. And truthfully he hated even thinking about it. After their last shared encounter, he'd worked hard on the mindful dreaming. Even if she accidentally slipped into his subconscious, he'd learned enough to slam that door hard. They hadn't had any shared dreamtime—erotic or not—for a month now. And frankly, that was just fine with him. He'd rather forget about the whole thing.

"Sorry, I forgot we don't talk about that," she said, echoing his own thoughts. "You don't even want to remember it."

"You're avoiding the subject, Christy." Which was a neat way of avoiding the dream subject. "Why can't you believe you'd get a good guy—summer romance or not?"

"A good guy, you bet. I've dated dozens of them. You know, the kind who's balding, with a good sense of humor, and is solid father material. Back in Ohio, I got fixed up with them all the time."

He winced. Did she mean that he wasn't solid father material? Meanwhile, she was squeezing his arms.

"But a guy who could pose in a calendar? Whose biceps are as impressive as his abs are sculpted?"

"You're saying you want me for my body."

"I'm saying your body is incredible. And you're kind

and funny and a really good person. Which makes you a *great* guy. A catch. The kind that girls fight over and drape proudly on their arms. The kind that cougars shower with expensive toys. The kind that could have a model on their arm."

She was looking at his chest, and usually he kind of liked that. It often led to all sorts of fun, but this time he touched her chin, gently bringing her attention up to his eyes.

"You're saying you can't catch a great guy?"

"Not your kind of great."

"Wow, I never thought I'd have trouble convincing a woman that I'm not that great. Or that she deserved whatever great I am." Lord, he was getting tangled in his own words. "Christy, how is it that you don't know how amazing you are?"

She looked at him, her smile weak. "Do you want the whole psychological background? With my joint problem, I was never an athlete. And I've always been plump. That was the kiss of death as far as any of the cute guys went."

He nodded. She'd spent her childhood on one base after another. And on base, athleticism was prized. Among adults and among kids. "But you're fun, you're—"

"A great girl." She said it like she was a piece of old meat loaf. "Yeah, I know. The good friend. The shoulder to cry on. The ones chosen last for teams, but picked first when you wanted to ditch your babysitting job to go out with the football star."

He winced. "Was it that bad?"

She shook her head. "It was fine. It was normal for the unathletic girl. Look, I don't think I'm a geek or anything. I just never thought I'd be the one with the football star."

"Actually, I played soccer in high school."

She heaved an exaggerated sigh. "Well, then, that explains it. I'm not with the star quarterback. I'm with the running geek."

He laughed because he knew she meant him to. But then he touched her arm, drawing her eyes back to his. "I get it," he said. "For whatever deep-seated emotional reasons, you never saw yourself as the prom queen."

"I never even made her court."

"Right. 'Cause teenagers are stupid, and high school scars us all in one way or another."

She opened her mouth to say something but he pressed his fingers to her lips.

"So the way I see it, you can either brood on the I-can't-believe-he's-here—"

She pushed away his hand. "I wasn't brooding! I was…surprised. Repeatedly."

"Either way, you can keep getting surprised, or you can get over your trauma. Christy, you creep me out when you look at me like that. Hell, you deserve way better than me—"

"Now who's got the self-esteem issues?"

He grimaced. "Touché. The point is, we both deserve this time together. We both are awesome. And if you spend all your time in shock that we're together—"

"We'll waste the time we have?"

He nodded.

She nodded, too. And then they stared at each other for a long, long time. It was weird. They'd just had one of those awkward personal, soul-exploration-type talks that normally had him running for the nearest beer.

But he wasn't running. He was just looking at her. And feeling grateful for this moment in time. Which made it absolutely perfect in some incomprehensible way.

"So, you just going to stare at me, marine? Or are you going to find a way to express our mutual awesomeness?"

He grinned, but then he remembered where they were. "I thought we had to be respectable."

She sighed, her gaze going back over his shoulder to where the luau would be. Then her gaze cut back up the beach to a semi-secluded area where massage tables were set up. The building had huge windows that usually let in a breeze, but was locked up tight right now. "Screw respectable. I don't have to chaperone until the sock hop tonight." Then she flashed him a mischievous smile. "How are you with a lock pick?"

He arched his brows. "I'm a marine. We don't pick locks. We break them."

She laughed. "Well, then, it's a good thing that I spent many a lonely night learning how to get into places I shouldn't have."

His eyes widened. "You didn't."

She pulled off her earring. "Had to do something when guys like you were playing football."

"Soccer."

They both said the next word together: "Whatever." Then a moment later they were inside the massage hut and he could finally, amazingly, do what he'd been thinking about since she'd wrapped her tongue around his sundae spoon.

16

CHRISTY PUSHED her way inside the massage hut feeling a sense of wicked liberation grip her. Yes wicked, because she was breaking and entering. Wicked because she wasn't a kindergarten teacher at that moment—she was a woman on a summer fling in Hawaii with a hot stud of a marine by her side. And wicked because she didn't have to be good. And that was so freeing, she started giggling even as Jason shut the door behind them.

It was dark inside, but while Christy was still exploring her new freedom, Jason was finding matches and lighting the candles spaced throughout the room. Then they both took stock of the massage table, cheap stereo, and array of oils and…exercise tubing?

"What are those for?" Christy asked, pointing to the tubing.

"Probably for flexibility work," said Jason as he picked up the longest piece and tested the tensile strength of it. "Or maybe something else…" he said with a waggle of his eyebrows.

Christy leaned back against the table, stretching her

legs out in front of her as she gave him her best come-hither look. "Really? What else could it be for?"

He set down the tubing, then pulled a fifty out of his wallet and set it under the cheap stereo.

"What's that for?" she asked.

"Payment for any supplies I use."

Now that sounded interesting. And really honest. The little bit of guilt she felt at being a felon for picking the lock melted away. "Fifty bucks of massage oil sounds like a lot."

He nodded as he picked up the tubing. "True, but I'm not just going to use the oil." And with that he caught her up tight in his arms. She went willingly, of course. That was exactly where she wanted to be. Except that it didn't go as she'd expected.

His kiss was slow and sweet, not hard and demanding as she wanted. His lips brushed back and forth across hers. Just a slow tease until she nipped at him in frustration.

"You're wasting time, marine," she growled.

"Really?" Then he lifted the tubing and looped it across a ceiling beam. And to her shock, her right arm went up along with it.

She stared at her arm then up at the line of tubing. "You shackled my wrist," she said, stating the obvious. "How did you do that?" She peered closer at the knot, feeling very impressed by the way he had caught her. She tested the strength of the bond. If she really worked at it, there was enough give in the tubing for her to break free. But if she didn't want to escape, she didn't need to.

"Cool," she breathed.

"Really?" he asked, searching her face. "Because if you're not into this…"

She bit her lip, then opted for the truth. "Sexually, I think I've been at your mercy from the beginning, Jason." He grinned, and she rolled her eyes. Like he needed a bigger ego. "I'm sure I have a limit some-where, but—"

"You're not there yet?"

"Apparently not."

"Great." He quickly bound her other wrist, adjusting the tightness until he could step back and survey his handiwork. She did the same. She was held somewhat suspended from the beam above her head. The distance to the beam was generous so her arms weren't hurt, but she was definitely strung up in front of him. And the way he was looking at her made her entire body hum with awareness.

But then the damn man just stood there watching her. Of course, she had to check. Yup, his erection was already thick and obvious, despite his jean shorts and loose tee.

"Hey, marine," she called, trying to appear seduc-tive even though she was hanging there like a cluster of grapes. "Lose the clothes. The least you could do is give me a good view."

He arched a brow, then nodded, pulling off his tee. Wow. In candlelight, his skin just glowed. Rippling abs, lean waist, muscles everywhere. He was such a beautiful man. She looked up at him and smiled, sur-prised and grateful anew that he was hers, at least for a while.

He was just standing there watching her, his expression narrowed as he studied every inch of her. "What were you just thinking?"

She frowned, her gaze dropping to his still covered hips. "That you stopped undressing."

"Yeah, you're going to have to work for further nakedness from me."

"Work?" She jerked on the rubber shackles. "Not much I can do here."

"You can start by telling me the truth. What were you thinking just then?"

"That I want your shorts off." And his penis inside her, but she wasn't willing to say that yet.

"Your expression wasn't one of lust. It was...sad. Just a flash, but definitely sad."

She frowned, trying to remember. "Do you really want to bring the end of the summer into this now?"

He flinched. "No," he said softly. "No, I don't. But was that really what you were thinking?"

She shrugged, annoyed that he was going all serious on her when she was strung up before him. "You're beautiful, Jason. Ripped. Strong. Hot. And I *thought* you were about to do wicked things to me."

He flashed her a grin. "Still on the menu."

"So get to it, already!"

He shook his head. "So you think this is over between us the moment the summer ends?"

She shrugged. "Or before. The moment you remember."

"Yeah. But that just means I'll have to leave for a mission. Or a debriefing at a minimum."

She didn't like thinking of him on a mission, but that was all part of being a marine. Dangerous work saving the world. And she knew he was made to be a marine. She just didn't like thinking about it.

He touched her cheek, stroking his thumb across her skin until she met his gaze. "Missions finish. Debriefings don't last forever. The summer doesn't have to be the end of us. Why aren't you thinking forever with me?"

"That wasn't the plan when we started."

He shrugged. "Screw what we agreed on. You're a forever kind of girl. And I believe I told you at the beginning that I'm a forever kind of guy. So why aren't you thinking forever with me?"

She looked away. This conversation was rapidly going in a direction she didn't like. "Things change, Jason. People feel one thing one minute, something else the next. It's okay. I understand."

He gently lifted her chin until she was looking again into his eyes. But he didn't speak. In the end, she was the one sputtering.

"It's okay, Jason," she said firmly. "Nothing's for sure in the world, least of all a summer romance."

"You got a guy waiting for you back in Ohio?"

She snorted. "All my guys are about six years old."

"And I got no one else either. We've been going great for a month now. What's stopping us from thinking longer? Most girls would have brought that up by now. But you don't talk about Ohio or anything beyond this week."

"*You* won't talk about anything beyond this week."

He acknowledged that with a nod. "But I will talk about a year from now. I've been thinking about that. About what I'll do after my memory returns. After all this is over."

She smiled and suddenly she wished she had the use of her hands. "You don't know what you'll want then. This was about staying in this moment today. Now. Shackled in a massage hut."

He glanced to where he'd set a bottle of oil in a warmer. "Oil's still heating. We got time."

When had he done that? She hadn't even noticed. Meanwhile, he was determined to push her. He stroked his thumb across her lower lip, but there was nothing sexual in the touch. More tender, but with an edge of frustration.

"Here's what I think," he said. "I think you have this idea that because I'm…hot—" he actually winced when he said the word "—that you can't hold my interest. That the minute things change in my life, I'm going to forget you ever existed. I might remember you fondly, but there's no way I'll pursue you after the summer."

She swallowed, startled by how accurately he had read her thoughts.

"That's insulting. You know that, right?"

She blinked, startled by his harsh tone.

"First off, you're the one judging me by my looks, not me."

"That's not what I meant, and you know it!"

"It *is* what you mean. I'm hot—"

"And smart, and kind, and funny, and, God, everything else that makes you the whole package. The real deal. The… Whatever other Hollywood phrase you want to drag out."

He took in her words without reacting. He just looked at her, mulling over her words, so she kept talking.

"Didn't we just go over this? I don't worship you, Jason. I know you have issues. Don't we all? But I'm not blind, either. You're a great guy."

"And you think I'm going to dump you two seconds after one of us leaves Hawaii."

She sighed. "Not on purpose. Not in a mean way."

"Because you aren't the kind of girl that could hold the attention of a guy like me."

She groaned in frustration, using it to cover the tears that had inexplicably flooded her eyes. No one liked their vulnerabilities exposed. He needed to just get on with the sex part or let her go.

"God, this just makes me want to shake you! Why can't you see what I see? Why don't you *know* at a core level how *hot* you are?"

She lifted her head, suddenly confused. Why was he mad at her?

"So let's ignore that you think I'm so shallow as to dump a girl because she's not as pretty as me, whatever the hell that means."

"I never said that."

"But you think it, and that's what's so insulting. Because let me tell you, if you were scarred or deformed or I don't know what, I would still want you."

She felt her face flush. That was good to hear. Really good to know that he saw her better points. That he knew she was more than just a chubby girl with bad joints. And of course, she already knew that. Intellectually, at least, because he was absolutely *not* that shallow. But it was still really good to hear him say it aloud.

"Thanks," she said.

Which made him curse and drop down on the massage table in disgust. "Wow, you really do have some self-esteem issues."

She laughed, though the sound was halfhearted at best. "Tell me something I don't know."

"Okay," he said slowly, as he stood up. "Okay, I will."

She looked at him. He would what?

"I will tell you something you don't know," he answered even though she hadn't asked. Then he stroked across her jaw before leaning in for the kiss she'd been waiting for. The deep kiss, the one that touched every part of her mouth, that said in the demanding press of his lips and the fierce thrust of his tongue that he wanted her. No question, no hesitation. He. Wanted. Her.

And then he pulled back and looked right into her eyes. "I'm going to tell you exactly what I like about your body. I get the feeling that you appreciate the great aspects of your character, of who you are as a person. But there are body issues here that have to be addressed."

"Do I have to be tied up while we do it?"

He beamed a telling smile. "Yeah, I think we do. Because if you're not restrained, I think you're going to distract me before I can say it."

She grimaced. "That doesn't sound like you're about to take off your shorts."

He shook his head. "Not yet. Like I said before, you're going to have to earn that."

"How?"

"By listening, Christy. Really hearing what I'm saying and letting it drop into your soul. Because every word is the God's honest truth."

She paused to process what he was saying, then she released a short laugh. "You are one intense marine, you know that?"

"Damn straight." And then he began.

He started with her face, which really wasn't where she wanted him to go. But then he started talking as he stroked her cheeks, and a kind of stillness entered her. Sure, his caress was erotic, and every second that passed had her heart beating harder and her blood simmering at a higher level. But his words had such a ring of honesty to them that they slipped into her soul and settled there. Deep inside. A place where no man had ever touched her before. She covered with silly quips, but truthfully every time he said something to her, she fell a little deeper in love with him.

"I really love your eyes," he said softly. "Your skin is nice, too, but sometimes the sun hits your eyes just right, and there's a kind of honey glow. Same with your hair."

"Like a cat's eye?" That sounded vaguely supernatural to her.

"No." He laughed. "More like highlights that pick up the sun. In your eyes."

She blinked, thinking that yes, she could believe her eyes were pretty. But he didn't stop there.

"Your mouth is great. Full lips. Easy smile. An easy woman to kiss."

She licked her lips, tempting him to do just that. He took the bait, nipping at her mouth in a quick tease rather than a full-on attack. Damn man. She wanted more, but he was taking this at his own pace.

He slid his hands to the necktie of her halter-top one-piece swimsuit. She'd never felt comfortable—or well-supported—in a two-piece. And there were too many ripples and bulges in her skin to go for a bikini. It didn't seem to matter to him as he undid the knot behind her neck and peeled the top down. He stopped long enough to get some heated oil on his hands, then he was finally cupping her breasts and she was sucking in her breath at how wonderful his hands felt. Big hands, a sure lift, and calluses that rubbed her nipples in just the right way.

"God, I love your breasts."

And in kind, she loved what he was doing to her. His hands were filled with her and he kept pinching her nipples between his forefingers and thumbs. But then he dropped to his knees before her, pressing kisses into her flesh along the way and she was too distracted to do anything but shiver in delight.

"You're like a WWII pinup. A bombshell. Makes me want to have you right here."

"Because I have big breasts?"

"Because you have *great* breasts." Then he finally expressed his appreciation the way she wanted. He lifted one to his mouth and began to suckle. He was an expert at that, the way he alternately rolled his tongue around, sucked, and even nipped at her. Endless variety, endless stimulation. Her knees grew weak and her head had fallen back. God, was it possible? Would she come just from breast play alone? She was so close....

And then he pulled back with a sigh. She was so annoyed that she leaped forward, trying to grab hold of him with her legs. He was too fast for her, catching her hips in his hands and holding her back with a chuckle.

"I'm not done yet," he said.

"Neither was I!" she cried.

His grin widened. "There's so much more of you that I want to appreciate, Christy."

She huffed and yanked on her shackles. The only thing she accomplished was to tighten the damn things. "Jason, please. Untie these. Let's—"

"No." Though still on his knees, he straightened enough to look up at her. "I want you to hear it all, Christy. I want you to *remember* this."

"Not a problem there, Jason."

He smiled. "Good, because there's more." Then he quickly unknotted her beach wrap and pulled it off. A moment later he had stripped her out of her swimsuit. She was now standing before him completely naked while he just stared. A few moments ago, she had desperately wanted to be naked with him, but now, she was starting to feel the blush heat her skin all the way down to her toes.

And all the while, he remained on his knees, his hands slipping down her rib cage to her waist. "Nice dip here."

"Not enough of one," she grumbled. Damn him for noticing how thick her waist was. If he thumbed her muffin top, she was going to kick him.

"What are you talking about?"

"Let's not belabor it, Jason. I know I need to lose a few pounds. More than a few—"

"God, you women and your pound here and pound theres." He surged up onto his feet then grabbed her hips, dragging her against him. Her legs had widened at his movement, and suddenly he was rubbing himself intimately against her. His jean shorts were between them, but there was no mistaking his erection. "Tiny waists don't look real to me. They sure as hell don't look like they'd stand up to a good breeze. Christy, you're solid. You're strong. Your waist is perfect!"

She blinked at the ferocity in his voice, temporarily stunned. It was ridiculous, but she really was shocked by his words. "You're serious. You don't see the weight at all, do you?"

She thought he would roll his eyes at her, but he didn't. His expression was quiet, serious and so honest that she nearly cried. "No, Christy, I don't see any weight on you, extra or otherwise. I see a real woman. One who is strong enough to chase after kids all day. Who is healthy and laughs often. And I see a woman with breasts that make my dick rock hard and legs that grip me just how I like it." Then he caught her face in his hands and pressed a long hot kiss to her mouth. When he pulled back, his words seemed to echo in the room. "Your body is perfect, Christy, but even if it wasn't, I see you. I want you."

She swallowed. That quiet core of her was rocked by his words. And if she hadn't worshipped him before, she was precariously close to doing so now. He wanted her. He didn't see the flaws in her body that seemed so glaring to her. She'd never really thought of herself as a vain person, but just hearing him say her body was perfect was like a giant weight lifted off her shoulders. Yes, he was beautiful. And yes, she didn't have to be beautiful back. But what if she was already beautiful to him? The idea was too amazing to believe. And yet part of her was listening. And whatever the truth was, she wanted him now like she'd never wanted another person in the world.

And she for damn certain was in love with him. Completely. Totally. Around the moon in love.

"If you're not naked and suited up in ten seconds, I'm going to kill you," she said.

He laughed, then shook his head, hideous man. "You don't get to dictate this today, Christy. You see, some time ago, you fulfilled one of my fantasies."

She huffed. "So shouldn't that mean you fulfill one of mine now?"

"Sure. Next time you can tie me up. But this time…" He took a deep breath and slid down her body again. "This time I get to force you to stand at attention."

She wasn't sure what he meant, but his movements were absolutely clear. She was just standing there, her arms raised above her head. But before she could do more than take a breath, suddenly he was on his knees before her and setting her thighs on his shoulders. It was a quick move, filled with confidence and clear pleasure. But it was also so abrupt that she had no time to resist or get shy. One second, he was standing in front of her all serious, the next second, she was spread wide before his mouth and he had begun licking.

Oh. My. God!

Long, slow strokes. Swirls and teases. He even pulled back to blow air on her sensitized flesh. She was writhing instantly. It was a good thing her weight was on his shoulders because she wasn't able to control herself at all. And God! He would not let her come!

Every time she got close, he would pull back and wait. Wait!

"Jason!" she begged.

"I never tire of hearing that."

She tightened her thighs. "I may strangle you!" Sadly, there wasn't a prayer of her hurting—

Yes!

A single long suck and she was coming in the most incredible orgasm. Her whole body contorted. And kept going as he prolonged it. She was gasping, screaming and dying all at once.

Hell, yes, she was in love.

And when he finally untied her hands, bent her over the massage table and sank straight into her, she knew she'd gone to heaven.

She could barely move, but she didn't need to. He was in her—hard and hot and thick—and she just wanted him stroking in and out of her for hours.

"More," she rasped.

"Thank God," he answered.

An hour later, he snagged a bottle of massage oil as they were stumbling out of the hut. "For later," he whispered.

"Wow, you are a god," she answered.

They laughed all the way back to the dance, where they held each other tight and absolutely no chaperone duties were executed.

And then that night at precisely 2:51 a.m., everything changed.

17

WHITE-HOT METAL SEARED through Jason's body and mind. He woke with a scream and a flail. He was fighting back, except you can't fight ghosts. Instead, he hit Christy's bedside table and her clock. His next jerk connected with her shoulder, and that more than anything woke him to full alertness.

"Ow!" she grumbled.

"Oh, my God, Christy! Are you all right?"

"I'm fine," she said as she rolled onto her back with a grunt. "Sleep-deprived, but fine." She glared at him. "You punch like a girl."

It was a lie, he knew. He'd clocked her good. Fortunately her recent workouts had built some muscle. She probably wouldn't even bruise, though he felt like a first-class jerk anyway.

He fumbled for the bedside table, righting the lamp. Picking up her travel clock. He'd broken it at precisely 2:51 a.m.

"I'll buy you another one."

"Another what?" She frowned. He held up her travel clock and the minute hand dropped to the floor. "Oh.

Right. Don't throw it out. I can use the gears and stuff for a collage."

He blinked at her. "I smash your alarm clock and all you can say is don't throw it out?" It amazed him how she could just roll with his punches. Literally.

She pushed up to a seated position, leaning back against the headboard. "Actually, I've got a lot of things to say. Are you ready to hear them?"

He doubted it. So he rolled out of bed and carefully set the busted clock on her desk. "Since when do you make collages?" It was a stalling technique, not that he really expected it to work.

"Since always. Lots of kindergarten teachers are into arts and crafts. It kind of comes with the territory." She pulled the sheet up to cover her very lovely breasts, then primly folded her arms across them. "Are you ready to talk yet?"

He winced. So much for stalling. "Um…let me hit the head first."

"Fine. But remember, you can run—"

"I'm not hiding!"

"Uh-huh."

He grimaced at her, then headed for the bathroom. Sadly, he couldn't stay there all night. But he could calm his racing heart, wash the cold sweat from his face and try to figure out what to say to her.

No go. He did manage to get calm and clean, but there was no magic solution for what she was about to say. In the end, he exited the bathroom and went to face the music.

"Okay. Hit me."

She frowned. "I'm not going to hit you—physically

or verbally. Your nightmares are getting worse. And more frequent. I'm worried."

He was, too, but he didn't say that. He simply shrugged.

"What does the therapist say?"

"That these things take time. Thank you, Dr. Obvious."

She tilted her head. "What do you think?"

He exhaled, trying to decide how much to tell her, then was startled by the fact that he wanted to tell her *everything*. When was the last time he'd felt that way? The desire to tell anyone everything he was thinking? Never. It was so shocking a revelation that he was dumbfounded for several moments.

"Um, Jason? You're staring at me."

"I'm…I'm thinking." He quickly averted his gaze. "I'm thinking that whatever I'm doing isn't working."

She raised her hands. "Hallelujah! So can we go back to what *was* working?"

He blinked, confused by her words. And then a moment later, he realized what she was saying. What she was *thinking:* shared dreaming.

"No, Christy. Hell, no."

"Why? Because it's woo woo?"

He grimaced. "Yeah. Exactly that."

"Too bad. Because the non woo woo isn't working."

He rubbed a hand over his face. "It doesn't make sense. We have rooms next to each other, and blammo, we're hanging out in each other's dreams?"

She pointed to the cinder-block wall. "Your bed is right on the other side of that wall. We've been lying next to each other from the moment we both got on base."

"So? I shared a room with my brother, doesn't mean we—"

"Who cares how it happened? It just did."

He stilled. "I care. And besides, it won't help. I don't even remember our shared whatevers." It was a lie, and he should have known he'd never get away with it.

"Bull. You remembered parade stance."

Boy, did he ever.

"And even if you don't remember, I do."

He gripped the sheets, feeling desperate enough to consider her words. But he couldn't. "Christy, there are classified things in my head. You can't see them."

She looked hurt by that. "You can't seriously think I'd tell anyone anything."

"That's not the point! It's *classified.*"

By her expression alone, he knew she understood. It wasn't about whether or not she would tell. The point was he couldn't tell. Not to someone without clearance. That's the way it worked.

"You know, you can control the dream. Just put it in your head beforehand that you won't show me anything classified."

"The entire mission was classified." That plus he really didn't want her to know that he'd been searching for a bioweapons factory. That's the kind of thing that gave people nightmares. Civilians didn't really need to know that kind of stuff. They weren't prepared for the fear that followed. But Christy wasn't deterred.

"A dirt track in some hot place with kids running around. Yeah, I'm sure I know a lot now about what you did."

He dropped his head back against the wall. She mirrored his position right beside him. Sadly, they weren't even touching. Just sitting there in the middle of the night running in circles.

Finally she sighed. "You're not getting better, Jason. If anything, you're getting worse."

"I know."

"Classified or not, woo woo or not, Jason, this was the only thing that was working."

"We don't know that it worked, Christy. Well, okay, the shared part worked, but it didn't help my memory at all. I still can't remember squat."

"Not true. You remember the village. The kids. The…" She shuddered. "The blowing-up, screaming part."

He took her hand, as much to comfort her as himself. Neither of them liked the "blowing-up, screaming part," as she put it. "But that's not what I have to remember."

"Fresh eyes, fresh perspective."

"From a dream?"

She gripped his hand. "Yes. A dream."

They sat there in silence for a long while. He listened to her breath and the steady beat of his heart. He felt her hand in his and the slow shift of her legs until she slid against his. Then she rolled against him, dropping her head on his shoulder.

"I'm going to stop fighting the dreams, Jason. You can still block me, but I'm going to stop fighting them."

He shifted to look more squarely at her. "You've been fighting the dreaming?"

She shrugged. "I put it in my head that we're not sharing dreams. That's all that's needed. It stopped me from even trying to slip in."

He narrowed his eyes, trying to see not her, but the

right path in front of him. "You say that like this is a normal conversation. Like this is a normal thing."

She lifted her head off his shoulder and he regretted the loss of her weight. "Maybe it is a normal thing. And if it's not, then why not be thankful for the gift?"

He swallowed. She was right. This could be some kind of gift. He didn't have any other explanation for it. But it still went against the grain of everything he believed about the world.

She tucked close to his side. "Just because it's weird doesn't mean it's bad. I mean, I'm weird, right?"

"Wrong."

"Okay, you're weird."

God, he loved the way they could bicker without any heat. "I am not!"

"All marines are weird, just in a macho, he-man kind of way."

"And all kindergarten teachers are weird in a fluffy kitten, hot chocolate cookie kind of way."

"That's not weird. That's special."

He stroked her cheek, leaning in close to kiss her. "No argument here. You are some kind of special." Their kiss went deep, slow, and had him rubbing long strokes against her thigh with his very hard dick.

She chuckled. "This part of your life works fine."

"I don't want to work on the broken part right now."

She licked his lip, then sucked it into her mouth. "Okay, marine. One quickie, but when I fall asleep, I'm going to hop into your nightmare and make it all better."

He pulled back, looking down into her eyes. "If only you could," he said in all seriousness.

"Let me try," she answered.

Instead of answering her, he rolled her onto her back then slipped between her legs. Within a moment, he was thrust deep and pulling out slow. Her eyelids fluttered, rolling back in that way she did when he entered her. Her gasps began with the second thrust.

God, he loved doing this to her. Seeing the way her skin flushed, the way her body opened so easily to him. He could spend his life doing this every night.

He stroked them both to climax. He tried to prolong it, made sure she enjoyed it. But he could only hold off so long, and at a certain point, he asked himself why he was waiting. Why stop the inevitable? Why fight giving her everything?

So she climaxed, and he tumbled right along after her.

By the time they'd fallen back into an exhausted sleep, he knew he'd just given in to more than sex. He'd given in to Christy. To everything she wanted, to everything they could do together. And he'd decided to give her his dreams. Even the nightmares.

CHRISTY KNEW she was dreaming the minute the sweltering air hit her face. Ugh. This was the reason she would never live in Florida.

She opened her eyes and looked down. Yup, bright yellow dress. She didn't know why Jason always dressed her in yellow in his dreams, but she had to admit she liked the dress. So she lifted her head and looked for her love.

"Christy! What are you doing here?"

She arched a brow. "I refuse to lose another clock to your flailing."

He frowned and blinked. She could see the awareness enter his eyes. Then he frowned. "You don't have another clock to break. I haven't bought you a new one yet."

"Fine, I'm here because I've gotten enough bruises. So, big guy, did you tell your subconscious to show me what you're forgetting?"

He stared at her. Guys always had that goofy look on their face when they were caught forgetting something obvious. Six years old or sixty, they still had that same "duh" expression.

"Never mind," she said with a laugh as she took his hand and started strolling. He had to juggle rifle and all, but in the end he took her hand and roughly shoved her behind him.

"It's dangerous here," he rasped. "You shouldn't be here."

She almost reminded him it was a dream, but decided not to. There was a fine line between being awake and being asleep. She didn't want to break the spell and have him wake up before they'd accomplished anything.

"I'll be careful," she said. "Besides, you're here to protect me."

He grabbed her face and stared hard at her. "I can't protect everyone. I make mistakes. I screw up."

She smiled, touching his face in kind. "I'll be careful. I promise."

He paled, his gaze sliding away as he scanned the environment. "I'd die if something happened to you. Christy, I think it would kill me."

She stilled, startled by his intensity. Her father had once told her that there's a crispness to battlefield emotions. The world is chaos, but inside, the feelings are burned in as if with a laser. The confusion, the fear, the agonizing boredom—all of it got etched inside with crystal clarity. Was this one of those emotions? Was this what she was sent here to see? That Jason was afraid for her? Or that he had a protective streak that was a mile wide?

She didn't know, and all she could do was file it away in her mind to remember later. That and to try to ease his anxiety.

"I'll be careful, Jason. I promise," she repeated.

He gave her a firm nod, then turned back to the road. She could see he was patrolling with other guys, but she couldn't see their faces clearly. She guessed they weren't important to her mission.

Good God, she thought with a bizarre giggle, she was even beginning to talk all military. Her with a mission. The idea was almost funny.

They made it to the end of the road in a split second. One breath she was stepping quietly behind Jason, the next they were coming on a school yard in a poor village. She watched the kids play because she was a teacher and that's what teachers did. One glance at Jason showed her that he was still scanning the environment. Still being protective, even among a bunch of kids.

There were some boys throwing a ball around. A ball or a stone, she couldn't really tell. Boys playing the kind of games that all boys did. One kid was running for the catch. He tripped, rolled over his own body like a puppy that was too large for his own feet, then scrambled back up with a sheepish grin on his face.

Being a teacher, she scanned his knees. Bloody but fine. He'd heal, though if she were at home, she'd insist on cleaning the wound. Disinfectant. Maybe check if he needed stitches. The usual.

She was just looking back at Jason when he faded from view. The scene simply dissolved away. She saw him turn and reach for her, a look of pain on his face. She tried to reach back, but his fingers slipped through her grasp. Then they were in the jeep and…boom!

She woke with a gasp. He came out of it a second later, flailing as was his new norm. At least she'd had time to slide out of his way this time.

He focused on her like a man zeroing in on a target, and then reality filtered in. She saw him take in the bedroom, process through that she'd been in his dream, and then he—

He punched the cinder-block wall.

"Jason!"

Her cry was drowned out by his cursing as he cradled his hand. Cinder block didn't give way to knuckles.

"What a waste of time!"

She arched a brow, waiting while he released his frustration in a few curses. He quieted soon enough, collapsing backward against the headboard hard enough to make her wince.

"Any other bright ideas, teacher?" he asked.

She tilted her head. "What makes you think that one didn't work?"

18

JASON FROWNED, searching through his memory, wondering if a miracle had happened and he hadn't noticed. Nope. He still didn't remember the location of the damn factory. The damn bioweapons factory that had been the whole purpose of his mission. He would have given up the search a long time ago—this tiptoeing through his brain was frustrating to say the least. But he knew he'd figured it out once before. Right before the IED blew, he'd been reaching for the satellite phone. Because he'd known the location.

And then blammo: Jason lost a piece of his mind. And his peace of mind along with it.

He looked at Christy, seeing the exhaustion dogging her eyes. Her shoulders were slumped, her hair was a disaster and there were bags graying the skin beneath her eyes. Waking up night after night to someone else's nightmares did that to a person.

He reached out, caressing her cheek, needing to feel the warmth and the softness that was Christy. She turned her face into his hand and pressed a kiss to his palm.

"If this were easy," she said, "you'd have figured it out already. We just have to assemble the clues."

"What clues?"

"The clues. The dreams. They're trying to tell us something. We just have to figure out what."

He let his hand drop away from her, but she didn't release him. She held him tight and brought his hand to her lap, right above where she was sitting cross-legged in front of him. He didn't even have to speak for her to know what he was thinking.

She smiled gently at him. "I know you've been trying to do this for weeks now. But you didn't have me on the case. Trust me when I say that this is no different than trying to figure out what a semiverbal five-year-old is trying to say."

He grimaced. "You did not just compare me to a kid barely out of diapers."

"No. I compared your subconscious to a kid barely out of diapers. And, by the way, I see that as an insult to the kid. At least the kid doesn't require me to be asleep and naked while we talk."

He snickered. A very mature thing to do…not. "Aren't you the one who said we have to use the tools we have?" He reached out to caress the sheet down off her fabulous breasts.

She batted his hand away and then slipped out of bed to grab her clothes. "So here's what we're going to do. You're going to buy me breakfast while we sort through the clues." She paused then turned to look at him. "Jason?"

"Hmm?"

"Are you watching me dress and fantasizing lewd things?"

He grinned. He loved how she could read his mind. Not that it was hard to read, given the tent pole he'd made beneath the sheet. Then, to prove that she was the absolutely perfect woman, her nipples tightened to little bullet points, perfect for sucking.

"Jason! I'm starving."

"Are not."

"Am too."

"But you're willing to wait."

She hesitated, her hands on her hips. She'd managed to pull on her shorts, but not clasp them, so there was an open V that showed carnation-pink underwear. It was adorable and he wanted to pull them off with his teeth.

"It's been what, three hours since our last distraction?"

He glanced at her clock only to remember that he'd broken it. "More like four."

"An eternity," she said drily.

He reached out a hand and easily drew her close. He caressed up her arm and gently urged her down toward him. But just as they were about to kiss, the sound of a stomach growling cut through the room. His stomach.

And instead of kissing him, she smiled. "Come on, marine. Time for chow."

"We marines are used to denying ourselves food in pursuit of a larger goal."

"Sex is not a larger goal."

"It is when it's sex with me."

She snorted. "No ego there."

"Hey! Just last night you called me a sex god!"

"I wasn't hungry then." Then she patted him on the cheek—like he was a sulky six-year-old—and stood up. A moment later her breasts were hidden beneath a very loud, kind of sexy Hawaiian shirt. "Choice time, Jason. I'm going to get some food. You can come or not, but I'm…"

Her voice trailed away when she realized he was already dressed.

"Damn, you marines are fast."

"Come on, I'll treat you to the Denny's up the street."

"Oh, how you splurge," she retorted as she grabbed her tote.

He paused, wondering if she was serious. He hadn't really thought about how little he'd spent on her. His tastes were rather simple. Coffee, eggs, toast. The local McDonald's was good for him. But maybe she wanted something better. She sure as hell deserved something better. "Uh, Christy…"

"Jeez, you're a pain this morning," she said. "Denny's, McDonald's, the snack bar, I don't care. Just feed me."

There was only one response to that and he gave it: "Yes, ma'am."

ON THE WAY to Denny's, he remembered a café one of his married buddies recommended. One quick phone call later, and he was driving her to a sweet little place with a terrace that looked out over the beach.

"We didn't have to go anywhere fancy, Jason," she said as she looked out over the waves.

"Do you like it?"

"I love it," she said, her gaze never shifting from the white stretch of sand and blue ocean beyond.

"Then we needed to come here. Besides, Eric says this place has the best hash browns ever."

"Well, then I guess this is money well spent."

It was because it was money spent with her. It still struck him how deeply he'd fallen for her. Looking around, he saw families here, complete with high chairs and grandparents. Three generations sharing a Sunday brunch. He could see doing this with her in a few years.

"Do you see your parents often?" he asked. "Your brothers?" He leaned forward, his chin on his hand. "What about Christmas? Big tree? Everyone singing carols around the fire?"

"With our voices? Hell, no. Beers and bullshit is more like it, but it's fun."

Over the past few weeks they'd shared family stories. His father was gone, thank God. He shuddered to think of introducing Christy to his drunken wreck of a father, but it would have been great for her to meet his mom. But she was gone, too. Which left his brother, who was off in Philadelphia going to school by day and being a bar bouncer by night. Not quite a Hallmark card kind of guy, but still, Jason ought to give him a call. And his sister who was a bigwig PR person in Chicago and often too busy to connect with him. But family was important. He needed to make a bigger effort.

"Do you want a large family?" he asked.

She arched her brows. "Wow, you *are* trying to avoid the dream discussion."

He shook his head. "No, I'm not."

"You've never asked about my future before. Certainly not if I wanted kids. I kinda felt like that topic was taboo."

"Because we're a summer fling?"

She nodded, and her eyes canted away.

He spent a moment mulling that over. Was he thinking about forever with Christy? Of course he was. He always thought about forever when he was with a girl. But with her it felt more real, somehow. Like it was actually doable, instead of a wished-for mirage.

"I like kids," he finally said. "And I think I'd like a couple kids." Then he touched her hand. "What about you?"

She flipped her hand over and caught his palm to palm. "I'm a kindergarten teacher, remember? Liking kids is a job requirement."

"Doesn't mean you want to come home to them."

"Doesn't mean I don't want a dozen."

He stilled. "You want a dozen babies?"

"Uh, no. Two, maybe three. Twins would be nice. With my joints, fewer pregnancies are probably better. But twins are a handful."

"Especially alone." He sighed. With his job, he was deployed most of the year. Time stateside was rare. Time with family, even more so.

"Military families have it tough." She lifted her chin as if challenging him. "But there's a whole support network in place. And it's easier with friends and a good husband, even if he is gone a lot of the time."

They were still holding hands, her warmth heating his skin, her strength bolstering his.

"I don't know that I could do that. Be away from my kids for months on end. I'd want to be there for the first skinned knee, the tea parties, and the baseball games."

"Internet keeps people in touch like never before."

"Even with high-res video, you still can't kiss a kid good-night. Kids need to be kissed good-night."

She nodded, her expression closed. They were still holding hands and her heat still warmed his body, but she'd withdrawn mentally. In the end, she slipped her hand out of his to pull a pad from her tote.

"Let's get back to the problem at hand, shall we?"

He nodded, though his mind was still back on the image of him and her at a Sunday brunch. A kid in a high chair to his right, another in a booster to his left. And maybe parents down on the end. A whole Norman Rockwell breakfast. The idea nearly brought tears to his eyes.

Fortunately, their omelets arrived before he could get too deep into his fantasies. She set her pad and pen aside and tucked into three-egg heaven. He focused on his hash browns like they were his next op. And before too long, the melancholy faded.

Must have worked for her, too, because her expression was open and relaxed by the time her omelet was gone. And then she was leaning back, sipping her coffee and looking at him expectantly.

"Yes?" he mumbled past his coffee.

"You ready?"

"Doubt it," he answered honestly. "But go ahead. Hit me."

"We're going to write down all the dreams. Look for clues or commonalities and go from there."

He shrugged. "Not so hard. I'm patrolling a dirt track. Sometimes you show up. Most times you don't. I get blown up. End of dream."

"Really? That's it? Didn't they teach you to pay attention to details in marine school?"

He all but rolled his eyes at her. "Of course they did but—"

"I'm talking about details, Jason. And not just of that dream. *All* the dreams."

He took a second to process that. His gaze slipped to the family one table over. The one that had elementary-aged kids and a toddler. "*All* of them? In detail?"

She flushed an adorable shade of pink. "Well, we don't actually have to say them out loud."

"But you're going to write it all down?"

She nodded and adjusted her pad of paper to a better angle. He could tell by her face that she wasn't about to be deterred. So he leaned back and tried to remember. The first dream wasn't so hard to recall.

"Okay. Parade stance. A personal favorite, I might add."

"No," she said as she started writing.

He looked up. "What?"

"That wasn't the first. It was the facial."

He thought back. Oh, crap. "Gee, how could I forget the one where I was a gender-ambiguous face guy?"

"Esthetician, and there was nothing gender-ambiguous about it." She looked up with a grin. "And by the way, that's a favorite of mine. Or would have been if I hadn't woken up so soon."

He tried to remember. Oh, yeah. He'd been going for her breasts when, bam, wide awake. "Okay, you got me there. But number two was parade rest."

"Got it. Three was your nightmare."

"As was number four. And we're done, right?"

She bit her lip, obviously thinking hard. "Yeah, I think that's it."

"So what do these have in common?"

She shook her head. "Nothing that I can see right now. So I guess that means we'll have to go into more detail."

He shifted on the seat, concentrating as he tried to remember details. It was hard. Like digging through sand, uncovering a little bit here while the debris covered an earlier part. They had to do it together, and they had to sit for long moments in silence as they sorted through their memories.

They had to leave the restaurant. They couldn't take up a table for that long on a Sunday morning. And besides, there were some details he really didn't want written down anywhere near an eight-year-old boy, stranger or not.

They kept at it all day as they wandered through the base, worked out, relaxed on the beach and ate dinner. It was evening when Christy finally called it quits.

"I give up. I have no idea what we're missing here."

"Welcome to my summer."

"Which means we'll have to do it again. Take another shot and see if I can figure out what we're missing."

He groaned. "Christy, you know I hate this."

"Yeah, yeah. I know. But you've got to give me a fair shake at this. One dream event is not enough."

"We've had four."

"Well, maybe five's the charm."

"And maybe we're just being ridiculous."

She tilted her head, her ponytail slipping sideways to flop over her shoulder. God, what he wouldn't give to see her do that in a cheerleader's outfit. He was so busy imagining that, that he didn't realize she'd been talking to him.

"Uh, what?"

"Uh, quit thinking with your dick and get ready for bed."

"Not the thing to say to get me to think of something else."

She laughed. "Jason! I'm exhausted. Let me get some sleep—dream-filled or not."

He nodded as he pushed to his feet. Hadn't he started this day thinking that she looked tired? "Fair enough. But don't blame me if our shared dreams turn out to be X-rated."

"Blame you? Hell, it's the only way to get you into bed before midnight."

"True enough. But that doesn't mean we can't—"

She threw her pillow at him. He dodged it easily, then he slipped around her chair to catch her in a full embrace. One hot kiss later, she was melting in his arms. One sweet hour later, and they were both asleep.

And dreaming...

19

"CHRISTY, IT'S DANGEROUS here!"

He saw her nod and step behind him. They were back in his dream again. On the dirt track that led up to the schoolhouse farther along the road. Then after that would be the IED and he'd be sweating himself awake again. Yes, he knew this was a dream. He also knew it was futile.

He wasn't going to figure out a damn thing here, but he had to go through the paces. She thought she could help him, and he wouldn't take that hope away from her. Besides, she was wearing her yellow sundress. For a glimpse of that yellow dress, he'd get blown up again and again.

So they started walking up the road. In the distance, he could already hear the kids playing.

"Wait a moment," she said, tugging on his sleeve.

He waited, turning back to her, more to see the light dance in her hair than anything else.

"How come there are kids in your dreams?"

"Because it's a school yard. There should be kids there."

"Yeah, but there are kids in *all* our dreams." She looked up at the building that served as the school. It was a huge cement thing, erected to be who knew what originally. But now it was a school. The teachers had hung up sheets to divide the rooms, and the kids had come. Meanwhile, Christy started walking toward it heedless of the risk.

"I didn't think about it because I dream kids all the time," she said. "But what about you? Do you ever dream about children?"

He tried to remember, but it was hard. This was his dream, and the compulsion to flow along with it was strong. Fortunately, she had more clarity. While he grabbed her arm and pulled her behind him, she just kept on talking.

"There were kids playing volleyball before parade rest."

He felt heat wash down his body and settle in his groin. Even in the middle of this dream, some words would always produce a happy face for him. *Parade rest* were those words for him.

"Were there children during my facial?"

God only knew. They were rounding the corner. Playground dead ahead.

"I think I heard kids playing. I don't know, Jason. Something about this just makes me think that kids are key."

"Kids are always key," he answered, though he had no idea where those words were coming from. It was just true.

She touched his sleeve. "What did you say?"

"Kids. The future. Seeing your children and grandchildren growing up in a better world. That's the whole point."

She arched a brow. "Can't argue with that."

Of course she couldn't. It was the whole reason he fought. Not for mom and apple pie, but for the kids. And the future. And here was that boy again, trying to catch the ball and tumbling onto his face.

"That cut looks deep," Christy commented as she left his side to walk after the kid. "He might need stitches."

"Christy! Stay with me."

She shook her head, moving easily out of reach. She'd made it to where the boy had taken his spill. Looking down, he watched her frown and kick at the dirt, revealing rusted iron.

"What is a metal grate doing here? Why would you put this on a playground?"

He stared at her feet, seeing the iron grate, processing through the information. "That's a ventilation grate," he said, his mind starting to click through the meaning. In the background, the world was beginning to fade. They were skipping ahead to the IED and she had to get out of here. But he kept staring at the grate.

Why would they put a ventilation grate on a playground? What were they ventilating?

The weapons factory. The goddamned bioweapons factory *beneath a school!* That's what he'd been trying so hard to remember. That was the answer!

The IED hit early or maybe it was just the fact that he'd found the answer. Either way, the entire dream world exploded in white.

He sat up with a gasp. Christy too, obviously jolted awake.

He looked at her, his mind clicking through everything he had to do now. Who he had to talk to. What had to happen now that they knew where to go.

"Jason?"

He touched her cheek, wishing he had the words to express his gratitude. He remembered. All because of her.

He kissed her. Hard, deep and with all the emotions that he couldn't express. Then he cut it off. He had to go. There was so much to do.

She looked at him, understanding filtering through her expression. "You remember," she said softly. "You figured it out."

He grinned. "*We* figured it out." Then he left.

Twenty-four hours later, he wasn't even in the same hemisphere.

20

OHIO HAD TURNED COLD in October. Christy worried about all those kids in thin Halloween costumes next week. She wondered if she'd made enough baked apple treats for her class. But most of all, she wondered if Jason was feeling the cold. Was he in a part of the world that got cold?

She sank lower in the bathwater, laying her head back against the edge of the tub. She let her eyes close as her mind spun slower and slower, circling the same topic she'd been obsessing over for months: Jason.

After he'd remembered whatever it was—she still hadn't a clue what—he'd left Hawaii while she was tutoring Judy. She came back to her quarters to find his room locked up. A day later, a young lieutenant had moved in and she'd known for sure that her summer fling was over.

But she kept hoping as long as she possibly could. In the end, she had to leave Hawaii. Her job in Ohio waited, and Jason was nowhere to be found.

She got her first email from him the day after she returned to Ohio. There was nothing personal in it.

Just "Hi, how are you? Are you still working out?" She could have gotten the same email from her brother, but it didn't matter. Jason was alive. She must have read those two lines a thousand times.

She wrote him back immediately. She'd meant to keep it light and nonpersonal, but line after line had poured out of her. In the end, she'd written him an epic of trivialities. The state of her apartment. Her dead plants. Her plans for the new school year. It all went into her letter to him.

Six days later she heard back. Again, nothing specific. Mostly he asked about what she had written. Had she gotten new plants? Were the kids good this year or terrible? Other questions, and absolutely nothing about himself. Worse, that was the last she'd heard from him. No email. Nothing for weeks now.

But it hadn't stopped her. She emailed him daily and was grateful when the address didn't bounce. And at night, she thought about him. And she prayed he'd visit her in his dreams.

Tonight she was doing what she often did: lying in a bathtub and dreaming of him. Her eyes drifted shut and she slid into a dream.

"You should light some candles."

"Jason!" She turned and smiled, seeing him standing there in his fatigues, his face dirty and his eyes alive with joy.

"I like this dream," he said as he crossed to the edge of her tub. "Though I do miss the yellow dress."

"I'm not dreaming," she lied. A part of her knew she'd fallen asleep in the tub and was imagining him here. Or maybe he was here in their shared dream way.

It didn't matter. He was here. He was alive. "Where are you?"

"Right here with you," he said as he knelt down beside her.

"Good answer," she said, shifting to kiss him. He didn't disappoint. He met her lips with a gentleness that was all him. Sweet, slow and thorough. That was Jason's kiss. And when the kiss ended she realized she was crying. "I miss you so much," she said. Or perhaps she didn't say the words out loud, but they seemed to echo in the dream room, infusing the very air with her loneliness.

She saw him react, his body stilling, his eyes widening. "Christy," he whispered. "I'm so sorry."

She didn't know what he meant by that. Sorry he left? Sorry he couldn't be with her now? Sorry she ached for him and...

His arm slipped around her neck, easing her sore muscles in a way that only he seemed able to do. She felt her shoulders relax and her back unclench. Muscles she hadn't even known were tight began to open up with his touch.

"How do you do that?" she asked.

"Long experience with heavy backpacks. Have you been lifting weights?"

"Worse. I've been decorating my classroom for Halloween."

He frowned. "Is it October already?"

"Where are you that you don't even know the month?"

"Shh," he whispered as he leaned forward to kiss her neck. She let him lave beneath her ear and then lower along her neck to her shoulder.

"Let me get out of the tub," she said though she didn't move. "We can go to the bed."

"No," he said. "It's best if I just stay like this. Just touch you."

"That's horribly one-sided, you know." She said the words. She even meant them. She wanted to touch him again, to stroke the morning beard along his jaw, to feel his weight on her again. But at the moment, just lying here in a warm bath with his hands…oh!

His hand had found her right breast. He knew just what she liked, knew how to mold and caress her, and how to pinch her nipple. She gasped and arched. What he was doing felt so good.

Still she reached out to touch his face. He pressed his cheek into her palm, but he didn't let her do anything more.

"Jason, let me—"

"Just stay right like that. We'll make this your version of parade rest."

She chuckled. "We'll call it Attention while Wet." And then she said nothing more as his mouth descended on her nipple. He pulled it into his mouth, sucking rhythmically while she gripped his bicep and moaned.

At first she didn't notice that his far hand was slipping down her stomach. Her breasts were swollen from his attention, her spine already arching as her belly tightened. No one else got her this hot this fast. And then she felt his fingers slip between her legs.

God she wanted it to go on forever.

"Jason," she managed to gasp. "Jason, come with me." She tugged on his T-shirt sleeve. This was a dream. He could climb into the tub with her. Or with a half second's thought, they could be naked in her bed.

But he didn't give her a half second to think. What he did was thrust a finger deep inside her. It wasn't enough. It wasn't him. And yet, she felt him there, thick and hard. As if it was more than just one finger. Ah hell, it was a dream. It could be anything. But mostly it was him. Thick and hard inside her. Stroking her to orgasm with a steady thrust.

He rubbed her clit with his thumb. He pushed inside her far enough that she felt it deep in her belly. And he kissed her.

The orgasm hit like thunder, rolling through her entire body.

She arched out as the wave hit.

Water sloshed everywhere.

Then her eyes popped open. She couldn't help it. Her body was still trembling, the contractions swamping her thoughts.

She woke.

Alone.

THANKSGIVING WITH HER FAMILY was exhausting, Christmas even more so. But she wouldn't have changed it for the world. By January's end, Christy had fallen into a depression. It wasn't unusual. A lot of people in the Midwest got depressed by the beginning of February.

She continued to email Jason. Every day, at least once. Because, hallelujah, he'd finally started emailing back regularly.

She learned the vague information that the bad guys had been caught, the bad thing destroyed, and that he was serving out the last of his deployment and would be getting out soon. He didn't specify what "soon" meant, and she didn't ask. In fact, every time she asked him about the future, about what his plans were after the military, she got a nonanswer.

He didn't know yet. He had feelers out. He was so buried in wrapping things up that he just didn't have time to figure things out. Or he just didn't answer at all, filling his emails with questions about her.

So Christy took it as a hint. She wasn't part of his plans. She'd been his summer fling and that was okay. Well, it wasn't exactly okay, but it was what they'd agreed upon. She emailed him a little less.

It was February, for heaven's sake. Time for her to make some decisions on her own. After all, that's why she'd gone to Hawaii in the first place. To try out some new things and to see if she liked the changes. Well, news flash—except for missing Jason, she did like switching things up. So it was time to start meeting life on her terms.

She didn't know exactly what that meant yet. She was being bolder about working out more, about not giving in to her limitations, and for damn sure not letting anyone—family or friends—coddle her physically. Blind dates with more bland guys were out. Stationary biking was in. And seafood. Lots of fruit and seafood.

But that didn't solve the heartache. The bone-deep I-miss-Jason that echoed through her heart and soul every minute. But she was learning to get past that, too.

And then he called her cell phone at 2:34 p.m. The connection was clear as a bell, which made her think that he was right next door. But he wasn't, because he commented that it was the middle of the night for him.

It was so great to hear his voice that she nearly

started bawling. It took her a little bit to figure out that he was worried about her. She hadn't emailed that day, and so he had to know she was all right.

They'd talked for seventeen minutes, and then he had to get off. His last words to her were "Soon, Christy, I promise."

Soon for what? He hadn't said, and she was too afraid to press. So she went back to emailing every day. What happened at school. What TV shows she was watching. How much snow was burying her car.

How could two people talk about everything and nothing for so long? And how long could she keep holding on when he couldn't even say when or if he was going to see her again?

March finally started and damned if she didn't want to just call it quits. Not with Jason, though the thought certainly crossed her mind. No, she wanted to quit Ohio. The weather sucked, the cold was murder on her joints and every disease known to kindergarteners was sweeping through the school. Sure, her resistance was high after years in the public school system, but she still spent way too much time wiping noses and sanitizing toys.

Then one cold Thursday evening, everything changed. After school, she'd had a school team meeting, then dinner with a friend who served her wine and patiently listened to Christy's whines. It was awful, but that was her life right now: limbo land with a guy who might or might not be alive. She hadn't had an email from him in three days. So she drank too much and moaned about her love life.

Her friend laughed, drove her home, and told her to either ask Jason point-blank exactly what his plans were or just cut it all off. Erotic dreams were one thing. But this was reality, and frankly, it sucked.

So she rounded the corner to her apartment while mentally composing a "laying it on the line" email. She'd write it up tonight, read it through in the morning, then hit Send. That was the plan. Except when she made it to her front door, a man stepped out from around the other corner. Not just any man, but Jason, looking drawn and thin, but oh, so good she just stared. She probably drooled, too, but as he was staring straight back at her, she figured it all equaled out.

He was the one who broke first.

"Hi, Christy."

"Hi, Jason." After composing nightly email epics to him, she ought to have better words now. No such luck. Apparently, in person all she had was the obvious.

"Hard day?" he asked.

"Long day. Then there was the drinking with Jo."

"Joe the principal's younger brother who wanted to go out on a blind date with you? Or Jo who teaches third grade and has a gluten allergy?"

"Gluten allergy. Fortunately it doesn't prevent her from getting soused with me."

His lips quirked at the edges. "Are you soused, Christy?"

She shook her head. "I've had either too little or too much. Don't know which yet."

He nodded slowly, his hand coming up to touch her cheek. God, it was real flesh against her skin. Real Jason. She closed her eyes and just let her entire body and soul feel his caress.

"Let me guess," he said. "You either want to be clearheaded and sober when we talk or so drunk that whatever happens can be blamed on the alcohol. Am I warm?"

She didn't even open her eyes. "You're hot and you know it."

"You're beautiful, and I want to kiss you so bad…"

She opened her eyes, her breath exhaling in a slow release. Some things were inevitable. Whatever was going to happen, wherever their relationship was headed, some things always worked between them. Kissing was one of them.

So she allowed herself to lean back against the door as she gave him a dreamy smile. Then his lips were on hers and she was feeling every part of him pressed against her. His hands were on her cheeks before sliding into her hair, his thighs were rock hard as they braced hers.

He was kissing her. Hard, deep and so thoroughly she felt as if she had sunk straight into Jason heaven. And when he pulled back, her heart was hammering fast like a freight train.

He dropped his forehead against hers. "Christy, can I come inside? Please?"

She felt he was asking about more than inside her apartment. He meant inside her body. Inside her heart. Inside…everything and everywhere.

She wanted to say yes. Yes to everything. To him. To his can't-talk-about-the-future attitude. To limbo-land for the rest of her life. But she was the new Christy right now. The one who embraced change, and that apparently meant staying strong against the man who once held her heart in his hands.

"No, Jason, you can't."

He blinked, obviously stunned. "But…Christy—"

"I'm not drunk enough to say yes to a man who can't pick up the freaking phone and call ahead. I'm not horny enough to open my body to a man who wants this moment and no more. And I sure as hell am not lonely enough to waste a year pining for a man who will talk with me for hours without giving up a piece of himself."

It was a lie. She was absolutely drunk enough, horny enough, and lonely enough. But she'd just resolved to stop living in limbo-land. She couldn't roll over now once she'd reached her limit.

He swallowed and took a slow step back. Her entire body tightened and it was all she could do to keep her hands at her sides and not haul him back.

"I deserve that," he said.

She nodded, her throat too tight to speak.

"So, Miss Christy Baker, now that I'm in town for a bit, would you do me a great honor and go out to dinner with me tomorrow night?"

"How long is 'a bit'?"

"What?"

"You said you're in town for a bit. How long is that?"

He shuffled his feet slightly and cleared his throat. Alarm bells went off in her head and she straightened.

"It's, well… It's a bit."

"Hours? Days? Weeks?"

He shrugged. "That's what I want to talk to you about. But I'm here at least a week."

She groaned. One week. One week with him and then what? Hell, she didn't even have time to get a substitute for tomorrow. "Why didn't you call me first?" she asked, hating the whining note in her voice.

"Hopped the first flight. Anything I could to get here as fast as I could."

She sighed. "Marines are supposed to plan ahead, you know."

"I'm not a marine anymore."

She blinked. She wasn't that drunk. She surely couldn't have heard that right. "You're a marine."

"I quit."

"I don't believe it."

"It's true. There's still some paperwork and stuff. Nothing happens in the military without red tape. But I'm done. I'm out. And..." He shrugged. "And I'm here asking you out on a date tomorrow night."

She didn't know what to think about that. So she reached for the most obvious thing to say. "I'm free tomorrow night."

"Can I come by here at six to pick you up?"

She smiled, her thoughts spinning through her schedule while simultaneously making plans for exactly what she would do and wear tomorrow night. "Tell you what. How about you come by at four? You can help me make chocolate chip cookies."

His eyes brightened considerably. "You're going to be making cookies tomorrow?"

She nodded. "Chocolate chip." There wasn't a marine on the planet who couldn't be seduced by warm chocolate chip cookies. She didn't know at what second she'd given up her hard stance about limbo-land and leaped straight to the best way to seduce him, but it had obviously happened. She'd already mentally mapped out a Betty Crocker kitchen seduction.

He cleared his throat and took a careful step back.

She might have worried about that except he had such a look of hunger on his face that she knew she had him.

"Um, that sounds like a fabulous idea. Do you need me to pick up anything? Flour? Chips? I don't know. What goes into cookies?"

She laughed. "I've got everything I need, thanks. Just show up by four."

"Can I come earlier?"

She smiled slowly. He sounded like some of her six-year-old boys angling for a treat. But she'd just spent the past nine freaking months waiting on him. He could wait a little bit on her.

"No, four o'clock's the best time, I think."

"Sixteen hundred. On the dot."

She snickered. "I thought you were out of the military."

"Honey, when it comes to you and chocolate chip cookies, I'll be whatever the hell you want." Then he gave her a sharp salute, a parade turn and made a crisp exit. Good thing, too, because if they'd bantered in the hallway two seconds longer, she'd have grabbed him by the collar and thrown him into her bedroom.

As it was, she had a few things to prepare first before she had her dream date with an ex-marine.

21

HE ARRIVED promptly at four. Christy expected nothing less and was actually ready for him. It was too cold for her yellow sundress, but she'd dressed in a soft blue sweater and dark jeans. Sadly, she wasn't the tidiest baker ever, and so she'd already spilled cookie mix onto her pants. She was trying to decide whether to change her clothes when the doorbell rang. No time now, so she threw the empty cookie mix boxes into the garbage, finger combed her hair and went to the door.

She opened it to a dozen roses and a gorgeous Jason grinning at her as he sniffed the air. "That smells incredible."

She'd timed it so that the first cookies would be coming out of the oven soon after he arrived. In fact, there went the timer bell.

"Oh! Gotta get those out of the oven," she said as she stepped back. "Come in. The kitchen is this way."

Then she turned around and tried to walk seductively to the kitchen. About halfway there, she gave up. Swinging her hips just wasn't how she moved—it was murder on the joints—so she went back to normal. She grabbed the mitts, popped open the oven, then pulled out the cookie sheets. And if she left her rear end a little high as she worked, well, this was a seduction. She had to do something.

She risked a peek behind her as she pulled out the second tray. He was looking. And grinning. And a hot wash of desire slid down her spine.

She put the cookies on the stove. Her cheeks had heated, not from the oven, but from him. She wondered if he could hear the loud beating of her heart.

"They have to cool for a bit," she said, stating the obvious.

He held out the roses. "These are for you." So okay, he wasn't the only one stuck saying the obvious.

"They're beautiful. Thank you." She buried her nose in the blooms, inhaling deeply. They smelled great, but mostly she was aware of him watching her. He looked amazing. He was wearing dark jeans and a button-down shirt with a sport coat. From a bulge in his pocket, she suspected he'd brought a rolled-up tie, but he wasn't wearing it right now. He was just standing there looking at her looking at him.

She straightened, feeling self-conscious. "There's a vase in the cabinet over the fridge. Do you mind…"

He was already reaching for it. Then there was water, cutting the stems and all the business of arranging the roses. It forced them to be shoulder to shoulder at the counter. His heat burned through her arm and made her mind conjure up all sorts of memories. It had been hot in Hawaii and they'd had ample time to explore every sweaty inch of each other. But this was the end of winter in Ohio, so she was soon stepping away to put the flowers on her kitchen table.

"So, you're, uh, making cookies for your class?" he asked.

"PTA, actually. It's my turn and I've got a world-famous recipe."

His eyebrows rose. "Really?"

"Sure." She pointed to the remaining cookie mix boxes. "Betty Crocker is known all over the world, right?"

He grinned. "Most definitely."

"I thought about trying to make them from scratch." She glanced at him. "You know, to prove my worthiness as a TV sitcom mom. But that just seemed like too much effort."

He frowned as he looked at her. Not a deep, what-the-hell-are-you-talking-about frown. More of a, my-what-an-interesting-thought frown. "You're trying to prove your worthiness?"

"You're the one with the sitcom family fantasy. Is it working?"

He nodded slowly, his eyes darkening with hunger. "Oh, yeah."

She flushed. "Good. Hold that thought."

His mouth opened slightly in shock. "Hold that thought?"

She laughed at his horrified tone. "Yeah, hold that thought." She quickly scooped up a pile of slightly cooled chocolate chip cookies, carefully setting them on a plate. Then when it was piled high, she offered them to him. "Here you go. Have some."

"Don't mind if I do," he said as he grabbed the plate and carefully set it aside, not even looking at it. Then he stalked forward, easily pinning her against the counter.

Her eyes widened and her breath stuttered, but her heart was hammering hard and she had no interest in escaping his hold. Part of her wanted to play hard to get. He'd kept her in limbo for an aeon, and now he was just going to show up and kiss her senseless?

Hell, yes!

He leaned in and she easily met his lips, stroking her tongue across his lower one. He made a sound deep in his throat as he grabbed her hips and lifted.

She gasped in surprise, her arms going to his shoulders to steady herself. Meanwhile, he was setting her gently on the counter.

"I had meant to go slow," he said.

"Yeah, me, too," she agreed as she wrapped her arms around his neck and pulled him closer. That required her to widen her legs so he could slide in between her knees.

Gee darn. He was there pressed tight against her groin. She watched his eyes darken and his nostrils flare. Better yet, she could hear his breath rasp as he stared at her mouth.

"Let me kiss you, Christy."

"Okay." She tilted her head just right for him. He claimed her mouth slowly, his lips clinging, his tongue teasing. She opened for him, tightening her arms so that he could deepen…everything. He complied, but carefully. And with such tenderness, he stole her breath away.

Wow. She thought time had made her exaggerate how good a kisser he was. If anything, she'd underestimated just how much she loved the way he stroked his way into her mouth. She toyed with him a bit, but in the end, he dominated there. Thrusting himself inside her, owning her mouth. Owning her body, too, if she were honest with herself. One kiss, and she was his.

He broke the kiss enough for them to breathe. His hands found her shoulders, but he didn't do more, and she had to swallow a mew of disappointment.

"Jason?"

"Slow. I wanted to go slow. There are things I wanted to talk to you about."

She nodded. "Yeah. Me, too."

He took a step back. "Okay. You first. What did you want to say?"

"Don't remember." She wrapped her legs around him and hauled him back tight. "You?"

"Haven't the foggiest."

And then he did the most wicked thing ever. He grabbed her hips and held her steady while he rubbed his thick, hot groin against her mons. They both had thick jeans on, but she felt every bump and hard ridge of him.

She groaned in delight.

He exhaled hard. "I'm going to come just from hearing that."

She blinked. "Seriously?"

He thrust against her and she gasped. Then his head dropped back as he lowered enough to position himself correctly before pushing another long hard stroke upward. She didn't know what sound she made then, she wasn't paying attention. But when he stopped, he was grinning.

"Oh, yeah," he said. "Could definitely happen."

She giggled. She always felt sexy around him. Marilyn Monroe sexy, and that just made everything more fun.

"Okay, big boy," she said, trying a Marilyn Monroe voice. "Do we fulfill fantasy first or strive for rational thought?"

He took a breath and she could feel the tension ripple through his back. "Your choice, but I know what I'd pick."

She did, too, and so she exhaled in mock distress. "Oh, my, sitcom husband. I've spent all day running after children and baking cookies. I'm just so hot in this kitchen. I think I'm going to have to take off some clothes to cool off."

"Here, let me help." He laughed, but that didn't stop him from stripping her sweater right off her body. "So in this fantasy of ours, where are the kids?"

"The movies," she said as she popped her bra clasp and tossed it aside.

"Thank God," he breathed as he lifted her breasts.

She let her head drop against the cabinet, then arched her back as she reveled in what he was doing. Fingers, lips, tongue; he was the best.

The tension was building in her belly. Her bottom started tightening, pushing her rhythmically against him. His mouth dropped lower to her belly, and she moved a hand to adjust her weight. But she wasn't paying attention. And *blam,* she dropped her hand straight onto the warm cookies.

They were just the right temperature, hot and gooey as the chocolate slid around her fingers.

"Oh!" she cried. "Oh, hell!"

He stopped what he was doing, which made everything worse, then he started laughing as she lifted her palm up to show him the chocolate-covered mess.

"Well, crap," she groaned. "I'm pretty sure that never happened on TV."

"I'm pretty sure I don't care," he answered as he took her hand in his and lifted it up to his mouth.

"Oh, you are not going to get disgusting with my cookies."

He licked across her palm and she shivered. That was weirdly erotic. Especially when he sucked her index finger into his mouth and tongued all the way to the base. Then he slowly slid her finger out.

"Was that disgusting?" he asked.

She shook her head. "Oddly not."

"Good. Because I like your cookies." Then he sucked in another finger, licking slowly, his tongue playful as he touched every inch.

She watched him do it, seeing the way his eyes closed as he tasted, watching where her finger disappeared into his mouth. She flashed on the sight of him entering her.

She touched his cheek, stroked her fingers into his hair, but her eyes never left his mouth as he licked every one of her fingers clean.

Then she leaned forward, embarrassed by her request, still needing to tell him. But in a whisper. She kissed along his temple to his cheekbone, then pressed her lips near his ear.

"Jason?" she whispered. "Can we do one of my fantasies?"

He stopped and looked deeply into her eyes. "Anything."

So she whispered what she wanted, embarrassed but beyond thrilled. "I want to watch you."

He grinned. "Your hand is all sticky," he said. "Let me help you undress."

He lifted her off the counter, then kissed his way back down her front. And while he was nuzzling her belly, his fingers unbuttoned her jeans and pulled down the zipper. She was already keyed up, already excited beyond measure. But as the zipper went down, so too did her inhibitions. She was with a great guy who wasn't intimidated or threatened or grossed out by her thoughts. So why should she apologize for what she wanted to do?

She shimmied out of her jeans, then stood there in front of him, completely naked while he was nearly all dressed. She reached out, quickly unbuttoning his shirt. He'd shed the sport jacket earlier, so with a few tugs, he was naked from the waist up.

"Better?" he asked her.

She nodded, loving the sight of him. Part of her noticed that he had bulked out a bit. Whatever he had been doing these past months, it had required strength without adding fat. If anything he was leaner than he'd been in Hawaii. Which made him especially gorgeous.

But she also saw a fresh scar along his rib that was maybe an inch long. She touched it lightly. "That's new," she said.

He frowned and looked down. "Oh, that. Training accident."

She grimaced. "Was not."

He chuckled and drew her fingers to his lips to kiss them. "I swear. It was."

"Did it hurt?"

"Not nearly as much as nine months away from you."

She sobered. That pain she understood well. "Jason—"

"Not yet," he said. "Not yet," he repeated before he thrust his tongue into her mouth. And when he finished with her mouth, he looked back into her eyes. "Is that okay?"

She nodded. "Yeah."

"Good. Because I'm hungry." And with that, he lifted her back up onto the counter. He made sure her hands were braced. And then he stepped between her legs and flashed her a grin. "God, you're luscious."

"Luscious?" she asked. "That's a bigger word than I usually hear."

He chuckled as he began to fondle her breasts. "I enjoy an adult vocabulary."

She let her head drop back, feeling happy and beautiful and scrumptious all at once. No one else made her feel like this. But as he began kissing down her belly, her abdomen tightened. She looked down, her eyes following his path.

She swallowed, feeling his fingers gently widen her thighs. "Do you, uh, want whipped cream or something?" She felt her face go hot.

He slipped his tongue between her folds and she gasped, every muscle tightened in delight. "Just you, Christy. I just want you."

And then he began.

She thought she'd be embarrassed. She was, kind of. But she also couldn't stop watching. She had a makeup mirror on the counter for those days when she was running late. She could drink coffee and put on her makeup at the same time. She was able to grab that and angle it just right.

And God, the feelings he was creating in her. He spread her open and bent his head. Her blood was rushing in her ears, her heart pounding, but she couldn't stop watching.

The wave was building. She could barely keep herself on the counter.

"Jason!" she moaned.

She tried not to climax. She wanted to wait, but…

"Oh, God!"

The wave hit, shocking her like a giant tidal wave. He kept her safe. Without him, she would have tumbled off the counter. But he held her still while her body went wild. And when she recovered enough to support her own weight, she pulled his face to hers.

"You. Now. Please."

He didn't need to be prompted again. He produced a condom out of his pocket, had his pants down and was rolling it on in record time. She braced herself as best she could, and then she got to do it again. She got to watch him enter her. She saw his thick, hard penis as he slowly pushed inside her. She watched his abdominal muscles ripple as he controlled his motions. And then she watched his length disappear as he fully pressed himself into her.

She kissed him. Once, deeply. Putting as much feeling into that kiss as she could. But then she pulled back, wanting to watch him again. He must have understood, because he braced himself and slid back out again.

"Beautiful," she murmured. Never would she have thought she'd be turned on by the sight, but she was.

Back in. Disappearing inside her. She felt him, too, thick and hard. She loved the fullness of him.

"I'm not going to last," he rasped against her ear.

"It's okay," she returned, but she didn't stop watching.

Out again. Then back in. Faster this time.

He groaned as he pulled back one last time, then he slid all the way home. She didn't think she'd orgasm again so soon, but he ground against her, and soon she tumbled over the edge.

It wasn't as explosive as the first time, but damn, it was good. He was good.

"I love you," she whispered.

"Me, too," he answered.

22

CHRISTY STARED AT HIM. Her heart was still thundering, her body precariously perched on her countertop. And he was still there, pulsing inside her.

"Me, too? That's what you've got—me, too?"

He lifted his head. His skin was still flushed, and his eyes focused on her with a kind of doe-eyed confusion.

"No blood in my brain. Give me a second."

She pressed a kiss to his forehead. Then another to his cheek. Then he turned his head and they kissed for real and for a long time. But in the end, she stopped it with a sigh.

"I always seem to be waiting for you, Jason. And I gotta say, it's getting old."

He straightened up. "The waiting's over, Christy."

"Is it?" She pressed her hand to his cheek. "Because from where I'm sitting, it's just more of the same. Great same, but still—"

He held up his hand. "I think this is a conversation that requires clothing." He trailed a finger across her shoulder. "You're beautiful naked, but I don't want to screw this up. I need all my brain cells on something other than getting you into bed."

She kissed him, then pulled away his hand. "For the record, we don't seem to need a bed."

"Not helping."

"You're the one still inside me."

"You're the one still gripping me with your very strong legs."

She frowned. He was right. Her legs were still locked behind him. With conscious effort, she opened her legs and he stepped back. They had other things on the agenda right now. Two minutes later, he was buttoning up his shirt, while she poured cookie mix into a bowl.

"What are you doing?" he asked.

"I told you. My turn with the PTA." She glanced over at the mushed pile of cooled cookies on the table. "And I'm not taking that batch."

He chuckled. "No, I guess that wouldn't be appropriate."

"In so many ways."

He sat down across from her and dropped his chin on his palm. "So how can I help?"

She added ingredients with the efficiency of long-standing practice, then pushed the whole bowl at him along with a heavy wooden spoon.

"You can use those big muscles of yours to mix while I talk."

He glanced up. "Sounds ominous."

She snorted. "You just gave me one of the best orgasms of my life. How ominous could it be?"

He stilled. "The best? Really?"

"I said *one* of the best. And no, we're not going to

talk about your sexual prowess. We have another problem."

He nodded and started mixing the batter, but his
movements were slow and she knew he was thinking
hard. "So we have a problem."

She sighed and pulled up a kitchen stool, trying to
build her thoughts in her head but mostly just watching the movement of his muscles as he stirred.

But in the end, she had to talk. After all, she was
the one who started the discussion. "Remember back
in the massage hut?"

He grinned. "Oh, yeah."

She flushed. "Before the 'oh, yeah' part, you were
trying to convince me that I deserve you. That I deserve a great guy with a gorgeous body and all the love
and devotion I can find."

He looked up, his expression serious. "Yes." Nothing more. Just, yes.

"So I finally believe you. I finally believe that I deserve a guy to build a life with." She shifted on the
stool far enough to touch his arm. "It's not about the
muscles or the great sex, Jason. That whole summer
was about forcing myself to change, to stretch my
wings a little. But maybe it was my attitude that needed
the most change. I won't let anyone coddle me anymore, least of all myself. And that means I won't settle.
I need to plan a future with someone. I deserve someone who will think beyond tomorrow to next week,
next year, next twenty years."

"And you don't think you can have that with me?"

"I think that we've been emailing for months, and
you've never talked about what you're doing."

"It was classified."

"And now what is it?"

He swallowed and looked down.

"I'm also thinking that you quit the military and showed up on my door without a phone call or an email."

He sighed. "I didn't know what to say."

"How about 'I'm coming into town, can we meet for dinner?'"

He shook his head. "That's not what I wanted to ask."

She paused for a moment, forcibly stopping her thoughts from spinning out of control. But it was no use. Her mind just leaped to all sorts of things he could want to ask her—good and bad. But when he still didn't speak, she leaned back and folded her arms across her chest.

"I deserve a man who will make plans with me, Jason. Living for the moment worked in Hawaii, but it doesn't anymore."

He nodded, then pushed the bowl of cookie dough to her. "This mixed enough?"

She looked, disappointment coiling in her gut. Obviously he didn't intend to continue this conversation. "Yeah, it's fine. Thanks."

Then she stood up and grabbed the cookie sheets and another spoon. Her plan was to scoop up the dough and cover her tears at the same time.

But when she turned back, there was an open jewelers box with an old-style engagement ring on the table sitting next to the mixing bowl. She stopped dead in her tracks and barely kept herself from dropping the cookie trays.

Her gaze leaped to Jason, who picked up the ring

box and held it out to her. "I didn't email or phone because this is the kind of thing that should be done in person. And I didn't tell you I was coming because I was too afraid that you'd say no."

"No?"

"Yeah, like that you'd met someone else or was over the whole summer fling thing."

"I've been emailing you every day for months. Don't you think you'd have caught a clue if I was seeing someone else?"

He shrugged. "You'd be surprised what I can be clueless about."

She smiled and finally forced herself to set down the cookie trays before she dropped them. "Um…" she began, but he shook his head.

"Just hear me out. I told you before that I was a forever kind of guy. I meant it. I love you and I want to marry you. But I know it's too soon."

It *was* too soon. And yet, her heart told her that it was exactly soon enough. She wanted what he was offering. Wanted everything that that ring symbolized. But she kept her mouth shut and let him talk.

"I've been thinking a lot about my future. I'm out of the military, but there are private security things I could do. There are jobs out there for a guy like me. But I've been thinking of going back to school, and get an MBA or degree in architecture, I'm not sure which."

"Not exactly the same field."

He shrugged. "I was thinking a job of some sort, and start off with a couple classes at the community college just to get my feet wet. It's been a long time since I've been a student." He grinned. "And then, figure out what's next."

"That sounds like a reasonable plan." She bit her lip. He wasn't exactly talking about the engagement ring that still sat cradled in his palm.

"It is reasonable. But before I can figure out where I'm going to school, I have to settle in a city. And before I settle in a city, I need to know if it can be here with you or somewhere on the opposite side of the country while I nurse a broken heart."

"I don't plan on breaking your heart, Jason."

He exhaled. "That's good. Because I don't want it to be broken. And I want to stay right here with you."

She opened her mouth to say something but he held up his hand.

"Like I said, I know it's too soon to propose, but I need you to know that this is what I want. I want to marry you. I want to build a life and a future with you. But transitioning out of the military isn't easy, and I don't expect you to say yes before we get through that. Before *I* get through that."

"I just need you to talk to me about this stuff, Jason. I'm not saying you have to have things figured out. In fact, that's the opposite of what I'm saying. The idea is to figure stuff out *together.*"

He swallowed and looked down at the ring. "I know. But I've been holding on to secrets—dealing with classified stuff and the like—for so long, it's going to take some practice." He looked up into her eyes. "I'm going to need help with the sharing part."

"You mean the being-a-couple part? I help you, you help me. We talk about what we're thinking and planning."

He nodded slowly. "I swear to you that I'm trying. I want to do this, I want it to work between us."

She leaned forward and pulled the ring out of the box. She could already see that it was too small to fit on her finger, but that was okay. She held it up between them.

"You're right, it is too soon for a proposal. But I meant what I said earlier. I love you. I want to work this out, too. More than anything." She slipped the ring onto her pinkie. "So how about I keep this for now? Maybe get it sized while we figure some stuff out."

"I brought it because it was my grandmother's ring. But you can have a different setting, a bigger diamond, anything you like."

She smiled. "What I'd like is to finish with these cookies then go out to a lovely dinner where we can talk and plan and discuss to our hearts' content."

He grinned. "I'd like that. I'd like that a lot. But there's one more thing."

She looked up from where she was staring misty-eyed at the ring on her finger. "Yes?"

He stood up and crossed to her, wrapping an arm around her to pull her close. Then he touched her chin, drawing her eyes up to meet his. "I love you with everything I have, everything I am. The next few months could be a real struggle, but the love will never change. I love you and always will."

She melted against him. How could she not? That was everything she wanted to hear and more. He was leaning in for a kiss, but she held him off. She took one last look in his eyes before whispering…

"Yeah, me too."

Epilogue

Three Years Later

CHRISTY LET a smile ease over her face as she stretched muscles that weren't sore in a body that was fit and toned. A dream. Yeah! It had been months since she'd shared an erotic dream with her husband. There was no rhyme or reason to when they happened. They just did, and with less and less frequency, more's the pity. So both she and Jason had learned to enjoy them to the fullest when they happened.

She looked around her dream only to realize that she was standing in her own kitchen. Then she peered down at her very pregnant belly and experienced another jolt of surprise. This was a dream; she was sure of it. But there were some very serious impediments here to the "erotic" part.

"Hey there, sexy," Jason drawled from behind her.

She spun around to see him dressed as usual: dress pants, soft sweater. He was the hot new architect coming home from a day at the office, already dropping his portfolio as he grabbed a chocolate chip cookie from the counter. She had lived this exact scene in real life, so she had no trouble recognizing it now.

"Jason, this is a dream."

"Yeah," he said with a naughty grin.

"Jason, I'm eight months' pregnant and this is our kitchen."

His eyes crinkled at the corner. "Yeah."

"But this is our real life, Jason. I'm really pregnant and we're in our own kitchen!"

He handed her a hot cookie. "Feeling gypped?"

"Yes! We're supposed to be, I don't know, belly dancing in a sheik's tent or naked in a jungle pool beneath a waterfall."

He snorted. "Haven't we done those already?"

She considered this. It was hard to remember other dreams while in one. Meanwhile, he was stroking her arms in a sensual caress.

"Are your feet swollen? Your back aching?"

She pursed her lips. "Nope."

"And we're not in Ohio in the winter." He gestured out the window where the rolling waves of Hawaii crashed on the white sand.

She nodded grudgingly. "Okay, that's an improvement. But Jason, what happened to our *erotic* dream?"

He leaned down and kissed her very, very thoroughly.

"Mmm," she murmured. "Getting better, but come on. This is still our real life."

He pulled back enough to look deeply into her eyes and she felt her toes curl. It wasn't so much his expression—which was delightfully adoring—but it was the feel of the air, the texture of the dream. It was like she was living, breathing, *being* love. True love in every cell of her body. Love *was* the dream. And it was wonderful.

"Jason?"

"I just want you to know that this is the greatest dream ever. More than I'd ever imagined possible. More than I ever expected or thought I deserved. It's everything, Christy. You, the baby, our life. It's everything."

She touched his cheek. "Jason, it's our life."

"I know. Don't you get it? I don't need an erotic dream with you. I'm living it. Every moment, every day and every night. I love you, Christy."

"You're saying our life is a dream, literally."

"I'm saying I love you. Always. Every day a little more. Every night—"

"A lot more," she finished for him.

"Yeah," he breathed. "I love you."

"Yeah," she echoed. "I love you, too." Then she grabbed his hand. "But if real life is just as good as the dream—"

"Better."

"Okay, better. Then let's wake up."

He grinned before pressing a long sweet kiss to her lips. "I like the way you think," he said. Hand in hand, they walked out the door…and woke up.

And then came the erotic part.

* * * * *

PASSION

Harlequin® Blaze

COMING NEXT MONTH
AVAILABLE APRIL 24, 2012

#681 NOT JUST FRIENDS
The Wrong Bed
Kate Hoffmann

#682 COMING UP FOR AIR
Uniformly Hot!
Karen Foley

#683 NORTHERN FIRES
Alaskan Heat
Jennifer LaBrecque

#684 HER MAN ADVANTAGE
Double Overtime
Joanne Rock

#685 SIZZLE IN THE CITY
Flirting with Justice
Wendy Etherington

#686 BRINGING HOME A BACHELOR
All the Groom's Men
Karen Kendall

REQUEST YOUR FREE BOOKS!
2 FREE NOVELS PLUS 2 FREE GIFTS!

red-hot reads!

*Julia McKee and Adam Sutherland never got along
in college, but somehow, several years after graduation,
they got stuck sharing the same bed on a weekend getaway
with mutual friends. Can this very wrong bed suddenly
make everything right between them?*

**Read on for a sneak peek from
NOT JUST FRIENDS by Kate Hoffmann.**

Available May 2012, only from Harlequin® Blaze™.

"Do you remember the day we met?" Julia asked.

Adam groaned. "Oh, God, don't remind me. It was not my finest moment. My mind and my mouth were temporarily disengaged. I'd hoped you'd find me charming, but somehow, I don't think that was the case." He took her hand and pressed a kiss to her wrist, staring up at her with a teasing glint in his eyes.

Julia's gaze fixed on the spot where his lips warmed her skin. "Does that usually work on women?" she asked. "A little kiss on the wrist? And then the puppy-dog eyes?"

His smile faded. "You think I'm just playing you?"

"I've considered it," Julia said. But now that she saw the hurt expression on his face, she realized she'd been wrong.

She drew a deep breath and smiled. "I'm starving. Are you hungry?" Julia hopped out of bed, then grabbed his hand and pulled him up. "I can make us something to eat."

They wandered out to the kitchen, her hand still clasped in his, and when they reached the refrigerator, she pulled the door open and peered inside.

Grabbing a carton of eggs, she turned to face him. His hands were braced on either side of her body, holding the door open. Julia felt a shiver skitter over her skin.

COMING NEXT MONTH FROM

HARLEQUIN®

SPECIAL EDITION

Available August 19, 2014

#2353 MAVERICK FOR HIRE
Montana Mavericks: 20 Years in the Saddle! • by Leanne Banks
Nick Pritchett has a love 'em and leave 'em attitude...except when it comes to his best friend, Cecelia Clifton. When the pretty brunette insists on finding a beau, the hunky carpenter realizes that he can't lose Cecelia to another man. Nick may be Mr. Fix-It in Rust Creek Falls, but his BFF has done a number on his heart!

#2354 WEARING THE RANCHER'S RING
Men of the West • by Stella Bagwell
Cowboy Clancy Calhoun always had room for only one woman in his heart—his ex-fiancée, Olivia Parsons, who left him years ago. So when Olivia returns home to Nevada for work, Clancy is blown away. But can the handsome rancher simultaneously heal his wounded heart *and* convince Olivia to start a life together at long last?

#2355 A MATCH MADE BY BABY
The Mommy Club • by Karen Rose Smith
Adam Preston never worried about babies...that is, until he had his sister's infant to care for! Bewildered at his new responsibilities, Adam asks pediatrician Kaitlyn Foster for help. The good doctor is reluctant to give her assistance, but once she does, she just can't resist the bachelor and his adorable niece.

#2356 NOT JUST A COWBOY
Texas Rescue • by Caro Carson
Texan oil heiress Patricia Cargill is particular when it comes to her men, but there's just something about Luke Waterson she can't resist. Maybe it's that he's a drop-dead gorgeous rescue fireman and ranch hand! Luke, who lights long-dormant fires in Patricia, has also got his fair share of secrets. Can the cowboy charm the socialite into a happily-ever-after?

#2357 ONCE UPON A BRIDE
by Helen Lacey
Although she owns a bridal shop, Lauren Jakowski can't imagine herself taking the trip down the aisle anytime soon. In fact, she's sworn off men for the foreseeable future! But Cupid intervenes in the form of her new next-door neighbor, Gabe Vitali. Despite his tragic past, the cancer survivor might just be the key to Lauren's future.

#2358 HIS TEXAS FOREVER FAMILY
by Amy Woods
After a difficult divorce, art teacher Liam Campbell wants nothing more than to start anew in Peach Leaf, Texas. He's instantly captivated by his new boss, Paige Graham, but the lovely widow has placed romance on the back burner to care for her emotionally wounded young son and focus on her career. Still, as Liam bonds with the boy and his mother, a new family begins to blossom.

YOU CAN FIND MORE INFORMATION ON UPCOMING HARLEQUIN® TITLES, FREE EXCERPTS AND MORE AT WWW.HARLEQUIN.COM.

HSECNM0814

REQUEST YOUR FREE BOOKS!

2 FREE NOVELS PLUS 2 FREE GIFTS!

⊕ HARLEQUIN®

SPECIAL EDITION

Life, Love & Family

YES! Please send me 2 FREE Harlequin® Special Edition novels and my 2 FREE gifts (gifts are worth about $10). After receiving them, if I don't wish to receive any more books, I can return the shipping statement marked "cancel." If I don't cancel, I will receive 6 brand-new novels every month and be billed just $4.74 per book in the U.S. or $5.24 per book in Canada. That's a savings of at least 14% off the cover price! It's quite a bargain! Shipping and handling is just 50¢ per book in the U.S. and 75¢ per book in Canada.* I understand that accepting the 2 free books and gifts places me under no obligation to buy anything. I can always return a shipment and cancel at any time. Even if I never buy another book, the two free books and gifts are mine to keep forever.

235/335 HDN F45Y

Name _____ (PLEASE PRINT) _____

Address _____ Apt. # _____

City _____ State/Prov. _____ Zip/Postal Code _____

Signature (if under 18, a parent or guardian must sign) _____

Mail to the Harlequin® Reader Service:
IN U.S.A.: P.O. Box 1867, Buffalo, NY 14240-1867
IN CANADA: P.O. Box 609, Fort Erie, Ontario L2A 5X3

Want to try two free books from another line?
Call 1-800-873-8635 or visit www.ReaderService.com.

* Terms and prices subject to change without notice. Prices do not include applicable taxes. Sales tax applicable in N.Y. Canadian residents will be charged applicable taxes. Offer not valid in Quebec. This offer is limited to one order per household. Not valid for current subscribers to Harlequin Special Edition books. All orders subject to credit approval. Credit or debit balances in a customer's account(s) may be offset by any other outstanding balance owed by or to the customer. Please allow 4 to 6 weeks for delivery. Offer available while quantities last.

Your Privacy—The Harlequin® Reader Service is committed to protecting your privacy. Our Privacy Policy is available online at www.ReaderService.com or upon request from the Harlequin Reader Service.

We make a portion of our mailing list available to reputable third parties that offer products we believe may interest you. If you prefer that we not exchange your name with third parties, or if you wish to clarify or modify your communication preferences, please visit us at www.ReaderService.com/consumerschoice or write to us at Harlequin Reader Service Preference Service, P.O. Box 9062, Buffalo, NY 14269. Include your complete name and address.

HSE13R

Slowly, Adam bent toward her, touching his lips to hers. Julia had been kissed by her fair share of men, but it had never felt like this. Maybe it was the refrigerator sending cold air across her back. Or maybe it was just all the years that had passed between them and all the chances they'd avoided because of one silly slight on the day they'd met.

He drew back, then ran his hand over her cheek and smiled. "I've wanted to do that for eight years," he said.

Julia swallowed hard. "Eight?"

He nodded. "Since the moment I met you, Jules."

Find out what happens in NOT JUST FRIENDS by Kate Hoffmann.

Available May 2012, only from Harlequin® Blaze™.

HBEXP0412

Harlequin *Presents*®

Royalty has never been so scandalous!

THE
SANTINA
CROWN

When Crown Prince Alessandro of Santina proposes
to paparazzi favorite Allegra Jackson it promises
to be *the* social event of the decade!

Harlequin Presents® invites you to step into the decadent
playground of the world's rich and famous and rub shoulders
with royalty, sheikhs and glamorous socialites.

**Collect all 8 passionate tales written by *USA TODAY*
bestselling authors, beginning May 2012!**

The Price of Royal Duty by **Penny Jordan**(May)

The Sheikh's Heir by **Sharon Kendrick**(June)

Santina's Scandalous Princess by **Kate Hewitt**(July)

The Man Behind the Scars by **Caitlin Crews**(August)

Defying the Prince by **Sarah Morgan**(September)

Princess from the Shadows by **Maisey Yates**(October)

The Girl Nobody Wanted by **Lynn Raye Harris**(November)

Playing the Royal Game by **Carol Marinelli**(December)

HPI3066SC